White Paint on Her Forehead

a novel by

Nordica Francis

PublishAmerica
Baltimore

ISBN: 978-1-60749-814-8 (softcover)
ISBN: 978-1-4489-1362-6 (hardcover)
PUBLISHED BY PUBLISHAMERICA, LLLP
www.publishamerica.com
Baltimore

Printed in the United States of America

For Aunty Lou, who raised me alongside my parents, and loved me with a big, big heart. Thanks.

To Ayla aka Alex
Love,
[signature]

Book 1

Chapter 1

Cora: "All that glitters is not gold."

Maybe that's what Hell is like, I'm sitting here thinking. Not the fury of eternal flames and shrieks from the condemned souls who are burning up in them, but a nagging and constant unrest, or some kind of ever-present flutter inside your self that makes you a little sad all the time. Yes. That could be it.

The nagging, constant unrest resided just below the surface of Cora's consciousness. It wasn't so deep seated that it was part of a subconscious that made her act in unexplainable ways, fly into rages, or sink into depression; sometimes it waxed and sometimes it waned, but it was constant. In the daytime when she was busy about her life, it was a kind of a vague thing; almost not there. However, she was afraid of nighttime. She fell asleep easily enough, but would wake up three or four hours later, in the first hour or two after midnight, and her torment would begin. She felt it physically, too; like a deep, deep sadness in the middle of her chest that made her writhe beneath the sheets and grimace from the pain. No tears though.

There in the darkness, broken only by the Tiffany nightlight plugged in low down on the wall next to her dresser, Cora felt alone with that pain;

alone in the world; with nothing to grasp or clutch at. She felt a kind of desperation in her soul and really feared that the feeling would never go away. She imagined that drowning could feel something like that; in those last moments before the final gulp of water that stops your heart. She imagined the desperate feeling of drowning a lot, because her brother had died from drowning, at night in a dark ocean, and she constantly wondered what that had felt like for him. She was sure he had made valiant efforts at swimming; head to the left, right hand stroke, head to the right, gulp of water, left hand stroke, huge wave, gulp, weakness, fatigue, gulp, gulp, Oh, God, fading, one more try, again, *attempted* stroke, water, water, dead in the water.

On some nights, she remembered incidents in her childhood, like an insult from her mother and that major rejection from her father. Both incidents had surprised the daylights out of her and she never forgot them. Those memories weren't even hazy. She remembered them like they were yesterday, and now as an adult, Cora was sure they had set her up to feel never quite good enough for the rest of her life. She could point to circumstances in her life and decisions she had made that had definitely been influenced by what she thought of as the inadequate self-esteem factor; so many things.

There was also the single act of molestation by a family friend, but she had confronted the guy when she became an adult, and he had apologized and asked for forgiveness which she granted, so that was supposed to be water under the bridge, but maybe it wasn't.

According to the talk shows, that kind of thing scars you for life in subtle and not-so-subtle ways. There had been no penetration. He had just rubbed himself against her thigh as he straddled her in the big blue armchair in the living room, and kept doing it until he came. Her body was cool on the underside where the leather of the chair touched her, and hot on the top where his body connected with hers. When he finally stopped and took a deep breath and got off her, she fled upstairs to her room to wipe his discharge off her legs, although at the time she had no name for it. She must have been seven or eight, maybe.

I just knew it was white creamy stuff that had come from him and was now on me all over my thigh and a little on my panties too and I felt so dirty all over and I had to get it off me because it shouldn't have happened and I would not tell my parents because it was such a bad and dirty thing that I had done and it made me ashamed of myself and now I was a very bad girl and dirty all over and wrong for doing that bad thing and could never get clean and what if I couldn't get it off me or I got it off me but people still could tell I was bad and dirty and what would my parents and everyone think of me!

Cora had current issues, too, though nothing earth-shattering or even remotely visible to the people she interacted with at work, or socially. She was normal and happy by all and any standards. She had probably made a few bad decisions in the relationship department, but hadn't everyone? Every woman Cora knew well and didn't even know, or had heard tell all their business on TV to Oprah or some other talk show host they were meeting for the first time along with several million total strangers, had gotten involved with at least one man she never should have given the time of day, but of course, it seemed the only thing to do at the time. It was that laying down with the proverbial dog and waking up with fleas. Oh well! Hindsight is 20/20 vision. No point in crying over spilled milk; the same milk that was given for free so he saw no point in buying the cow.

Cora knew that if she was asked to pinpoint **the** source of her angst, she couldn't do it; couldn't put her finger on it. Somewhere inside herself she felt that no one thing was probably *the* thing that made her nights a living hell, so she figured it had to be the cumulative effect of all the issues; ghosts of issues past and present, which of course gave birth to ghosts of the future. What if she never got to experience joy and peace? What if she never found the almost-perfect relationship? Cora didn't think that the uncertainty about her future was a big player in her state of unrest, though. The future was mostly a long, black tunnel she couldn't see the other end of, so there was no point in looking in there. The culprit had to be her current thinking about her past and present, influenced as it was by the notions she'd been left with along the continuum of her life experience. She figured that the white man-black woman relationship issue was something else that bugged her most along with everything else, because she had gotten into one of those relationships when her feelings were neither here nor there on the black and white race relations matter, having not been directly exposed to that nonsense in her upbringing, and Oh! Did she have a baptism by fire! As Cora sat staring into the middle distance she thought:

Maybe my past, present, and future issues do weigh in as a package, or more accurately, as my baggage; some kind of emotional albatross to carry around the rest of my life. Or, maybe not an albatross. That was kind of a big bird that would get everyone's attention. Maybe I would carry an emotional scar; like a deep gash in the skin, that with time had closed, but hadn't healed completely, so that there remained a sliver of soft tissue down the middle of it that could rupture at any time and cause bleeding again—and pain. It would bleed and hurt and feel like it just happened.

Cora had been in therapy for a year not so long ago and had discussed her issues, especially the sexual molestation, but the therapist, whom she is calling Toby to protect his identity (God only knows why; he wasn't worth the salt in his body—with regard to his job, that is. All God's children deserved whatever share of salt they'd been given at birth; Cora knew this), had not been helpful. In fact, truth be told, the guy was useless. His comment about that incident in the blue armchair, and she couldn't remember now what it was at the time, was superficial and absent-minded; that much she remembered. She couldn't recall his words now, but she *could* recall the feeling of nothingness that wafted across the room from him over to her as she sat in the upholstered parson's chair directly across from him sitting in his un-reclined recliner. It should have struck her that they were sitting in adversarial positions; she had taken Psych 101, and she was sure it had crossed her mind and been dismissed as one more thing she was analyzing for no reason. There was a couch in the room, but Cora never wanted to be on that thing; never wanted to feel like she was actually seeing a shrink. She also recalled thinking that she could have discussed her issues with a girlfriend over a cup of coffee at Starbucks and gotten better results. The coffee would have been the same price as a session, since her insurance covered eighty percent of it, and the benefits from talking to her girlfriend would have been way better because her girlfriend would have said things that made real sense, like ***"You should pay someone to castrate the son of a bitch! It's not too late. Actually, I know someone, if you want…"*** Her girlfriend would have walked in her shoes for a moment and empathized with her—felt her pain, so to speak, and offered to do something about it.

Cora caught herself wrapped up in this stream of self-reflection, going back and forth between talking to herself and thinking of herself, and as it were, came to, and noticed that she was steaming with rage. She felt her nostrils flare as she began thinking about her own interracial relationship with Mike. She now shifted her gaze to her daughter, Julia, whom she could see from the porch of their beachfront home and felt her stomach churn with anger. Not that Julia had done anything wrong.

It was evening, and throngs of people strolled along the beach, but Cora's gaze was fixed on Julia. The girl's body formed a curvy silhouette as she sat on a low, wide rock that was right at the place where the surf stopped its rolling in. Julia was watching couples walk by barefoot at that very shallow part of the beach, mostly dressed in street clothes that were rolled up or hauled up out of the water's way. She let her own feet touch the water. Julia was a gorgeous girl, easy on the eyes, to borrow a phrase from—somewhere.

The girl reminded Cora of herself as a young woman. Like Julia now, Cora liked watching the interaction and playful dance between lovers and would-be-lovers from a distance. They took her back to her own teenage years of torrid sex and perpetual flirtation with men. Her daughter was now seventeen, elegant and tall, with legs that seemed to begin beneath her collar bone. Her curves were in all the right places, and she exuded grace and sensuality in the most casual of her movements. When she walked, she seemed to be doing some subtly suggestive dance. Women watched her with squinted eyes or from their peripheral vision, pretending not to be watching. Men watched her unabashedly, with parted lips and slightly accelerated breathing. Julia's shapeliness and flirtatious glances at men had not escaped her mother. Cora remembered her own voluptuous bosom, and the way she had used it as a young woman to win favors from members of the opposite sex. It had always gotten her a little something extra: a second glance from guys her age, a lustful nod from an older gentleman. She recalled the time an old man teetered and fell as he let go of his cane to wave, having caught sight of her coming in his direction, breasts bouncing as they led the way. The twinkle in his eye told her that there was a time, maybe not so long ago, when he would have stopped her in her tracks, found out where he could find her later, made a pass and tried to score. There were also the A's in Mr. Huey's Social Studies class—senior year in high school—when a C was really all she'd earned and a B would have been favor enough. Not that she couldn't have been an A student; she was a bright girl. She just didn't see the point in working for it if she could have it with no effort on her own part. The women she encountered had not been so free with their favors. Their eyes would make a quick descent from her face to her chest and back, bringing a noticeable tinge of *something* to their smile, and a suddenly inferior tone to their voice if they had to interact with her— either from an involuntary surge of jealousy, or something of an apology for sharing her space, for certainly the planet welcomed and graciously hosted such beautiful women, and was committed to a conspiracy that would make every phase of their lives a glorious symphony of eloquent passages. They knew without knowing anything about her that she had been cooed at as a baby by relatives and strangers alike, coddled a little longer at the breast, encouraged in every toddler endeavor. Why, the very poop in her pamper had been an amazing thing. Daddy always changed his darling little Cora without wrinkling his nose even once. That's the reason her father's sudden rejection of her one day when she started climbing onto his lap to play **Horsie** had thrown her for a loop. Dad had noticed that Cora was growing up, when she herself, was not yet aware of it, Cora later figured out. She still had her innocence intact, and thought nothing of these games. In her father's mind, however, being straddled by his daughter to play riding games was no longer appropriate. Her feelings were hurt. She thought she had suddenly become unworthy of her father's love; had done something that made him not like her anymore. Later in life she would experience warmth and love from men, only to have their feelings suddenly change for no apparent reason. Before the teenage cheerleading and beauty queen days, she had been a child star at school, adored by teachers and classmates. She was a little above average intelligence, not that that much, but folks generally thought she was a genius. Everyone knew who she was, and there was copious joy in their hearts that she shared with them the same space and time. She accepted their adoration as though it were her birthright, being neither cocky nor shy about receiving that much love and attention from everyone she encountered. Men were not trying to win her heart then. It was all about just loving her for herself. Cora's darling daughter, Julia, seemed to have inherited all of her mother's genetic gifts, including the blessings of a Double D bosom.

Now forty-six, Cora did not let her thoughts linger on those early days of grade school and high school, but instead thought about her early twenties. It was the period of her life when romantic liaisons moved beyond teenage team dating at the mall, or double-dating at the movies, to a need for exclusivity and privacy.

I had fallen in love uninfluenced by girlfriends, dated just him, and gave no one the details of my love life. My friends came to their own conclusions about my relationship with Mike, based solely on what they observed or imagined. I never discussed my relationship with anyone. I really didn't have a best friend as a teenager, or even in my early twenties, for that matter. Relationships with females were cordial, but superficial. I knew groups of girls who were close, but I was never a part of the clique. No one had invited me in, and I hadn't managed to get in as a matter of course. Nor did I want to. Back then, I was very comfortable in my own skin and in my own company. I would mention, only if asked, that I'd been away in Europe for a month, or was leaving shortly for a week in the Pacific Islands.

Cora had also noticed that questions about her love life would come up only when she stumbled into a group of women that she knew casually, but well enough to pause for a greeting. Then, they would interview her as a team. It was obvious to her even then that they just wanted in on her private life without caring much about her. That didn't bother her much, their not really caring about her. There were many other things that made her content. Cora knew she had good chances and opportunities for happiness and great success in her life. Apart from the little faux pas all parents make, her parents had given her the best of everything they had, and she had grown up confident and vivacious, expecting only good things to come her way, and for a while, only good things did. Now Julia seemed to exude the same self-confidence and feelings of entitlement to love and attention from everyone she met. Cora worried about that. She knew that life could change in a flash, and that one bad experience could ruin your sense of who you are and take away your self worth forever. Not that her own life was miserable now, but she harbored her share of painful memories, and a great despair that surfaced in the middle of the night as she lay alone in her bed. She was romantically involved now, and relatively happy when she was with her man, but never exuberant. She didn't feel joy deep down inside herself, and half expected things to sour at any time. Maybe it was because she knew that Clayton Sax was not her first choice as a lover or significant other. After losing the love of her life, Cora's heart had short-circuited, and shut her down emotionally.

I'm really at a place where I truly can't be bothered with love and feelings and stomach butterflies and all of that man-induced craziness.

Cora focused on setting small goals for herself and achieving them; decided she could be everything she would have liked to marry.

She had agreed to start a relationship with Clayton after eight months of a very casual friendship. He had immediately fallen in love with her the day they met at an outdoor concert, but Cora did not have feelings like that for him. It had been a beautiful evening in mid-July, she remembered. They had exchanged phone numbers, and after he had pursued her doggedly for several months, she agreed to an exclusive relationship with him only because she thought it would be a shame to reject that much love. Besides, who else was there? He was very obviously taken with her, and would make her a good husband if she ever decided to go that far with him. In a way, she felt that she was settling because she really wasn't feeling much of anything for him, but there was no real harm that could come from being with him, and maybe she, too, would eventually fall in love, making it all okay in the end. For one thing, the relationship was easy to manage. They didn't attract attention when they went out in public the way her relationship with Mike had, and certainly he was happy to have her around his friends and relatives. That was new for her, and somewhat comforting. The white man to whom she had given her heart and whom she truly loved, *that Mike person*, had been ashamed of her because she was black. The relationship had lasted only because she was so much in love with him, and there were no overtly unpleasant experiences. However, the self-loathing she felt from his hiding her from his friends and family sickened her soul, and killed her spirit. She would eventually bow gracefully out of the relationship in order to retain her dignity, but she hurt every day from missing him, and wondered whom he would choose to replace her. Would he fall in love, or would he marry '*her*' because she blended well with his family when they gathered? His brother's girlfriend blended in. She was white.

Bernadette, Mike's mother, was eager to have a grandchild. She was very ill from complications of diabetes and could die at any time. So Mike said. He thought, and said, it would be nice to make her happy by giving her a grandchild she could spoil before she left the face of the earth. She had seen him buy his first house and she was "happy, happy, happy," to use his own words. Would *she* pick the girl? She was used to finding him ads in the Singles section of the newspaper on a weekly basis. He had not shown any interest in that at the time, but she kept up her efforts on his behalf because he had never told her that he was in a relationship with someone. As far as his mother knew, there was no woman in his life, and he needed one. Cora had overheard several of their phone conversations as she waited for him to hang up and return his attention to her:

"I'm not interested Ma."

"_____"

"Oh, yeah?"

"_____,"

"Ma, please. Stop. You're killing me."

He had always returned to Cora with, "My mother's trying to fix me up again." Cora would smile, but say nothing one way or the other. Now that she looked at everything in retrospect, she wondered if having an angry fit would have been the thing to do. Should she have made sure he told his mother there was already a woman in his life and demanded an introduction? Should she have told his mother herself? He had once suggested she do just that and she had thought it was a stupid idea, but desperate times call for desperate measures. It might have been the thing to do. She couldn't fix it now. That window of opportunity, to coin a favorite phrase of prosecution attorneys, had been permanently closed.

Now this situation with my daughter... As much as I'm happy that Julia is well liked by everyone who meets her, and as much as I am proud of my daughter's good looks and self-confidence, I feel compelled to make every effort to protect my only child from the kinds of experiences that had scarred my own soul as a young woman. Specifically, very specifically, I feel that I need to protect Julia from white men in the still so racist society that is America. Never mind the fact that they had just elected a black president. There was still a little band of TV personalities who couldn't wait for him to fail, and newspapers coming up with asinine cartoons.

Thinking about Julia and Charlie, her daughter's caucasian hunk of a guy, forced Cora to recall the deep sadness she had suffered through years of a relationship that had chipped away at her self-esteem little by little. Julia was a girl with joie de vivre, and would soon, as nature's course would have it, want to experience the joys of sexual intercourse. Cora was okay with thinking of her daughter as someday having sexual intercourse.

She couldn't bear the thought of her daughter fucking or being fucked by anyone, especially not by a white man.

Cora reminisced that in the beginning of her own interracial relationship, she had suffered not at all. In fact, she felt that she had actually accomplished something, and was worthy of no less. Mike was her parents' reward for raising their daughter as they had. It was not because he was white that Cora loved him, but because his values seemed closer to hers, both of them having been raised by professional parents in an upper middle class household. However, in the end it would turn out to be all about race. She hadn't known that then. What she knew at the time was that he loved books and travel like she did. They enjoyed the theatre and went antiquing together. He also never came to her house expecting that she had cooked some meal he could dive into. She had heard stories of men walking into their girlfriends' houses, and going straight into their kitchens to see what they had cooked. Cora thought that was funny, and could not imagine herself ever being in that situation.

A guy could probably do that to me one time, when I had no idea he could do that, but just once. I would immediately be done with him after **that.**

If Mike and Cora were going to have dinner, they'd be eating out, except she really wanted to make him something special, which she did from time to time. Cora hated feeling that anything was expected of her, or that she had some duty to do certain things. She had seen enough talk shows where women complained about being taken for granted by the men in their lives. Left to herself, Cora would do anything for her man, but he couldn't come over, or come home, demanding or expecting whatever it was he was demanding or expecting. The men she had met pre-Mike had been wrong for her on many levels. Now she thought she had broken away from their circles once and for all. She held Mike dear to her heart. The men that she encountered now got only the most fleeting of her glances; a virtual dismissal.

I had not envisioned a future with marriage and children.

In fact, Mike had told me not to expect it, but I thought I had found my prince.

Later Cora would recognize that first honest remark as the cue she should have taken to discontinue the relationship with him; but with blinders on she had gone full steam ahead, telling herself that she wasn't interested in marriage and children anyway. How many relationships was she going to end because of something casually said or done by a guy? She actually felt privileged to be dating Mike. Her friends, as casually connected to her as they were, were always casting remarks about other friends who had had another breakup. Cora had been known to quickly break off a few relationships herself, and was now beginning to feel second rate, a notch below, despite her privileged upbringing and education. She would have to prove to herself that nothing was wrong with her, that she could get and keep a man as well as any other woman could. So she dug in and dug in deep. She resolved to give him all or nothing. Looking back now, she knew she had given him all for nothing; knew that he was never really deserving of her. *He* had been the privileged partner, and *she* had given up way too much.

Charlie, Julia's heartthrob, reminded Cora of Mike in many ways: The tall lean body, the striking good looks, the mop of hair (though his was blonde not black) atop the deep blue eyes, and the greatest pair of legs in the world. Cora had seen and read much; understood the tendency of children, especially daughters, to repeat the mistakes of their parents—maybe because parents' fears that their children would follow in their footsteps were silently communicated every day and in every way; and communicated so clearly that it would be all the child would want to do. *Why is Charlie interested in my daughter?* Cora wondered aloud. Had he ever been with a woman of color? Black men with white women were a pretty common sight on the promenade, and for that matter everywhere else, but white men had not begun to "cross over" as Cora liked to put it. Cora thought there was, generally speaking, no pattern in white men's lives of dating black women, although even that rule had its exceptions, she was sure, and lately there were a few of those couples on TV, too. But judging by what she had seen of interracial dating in her everyday life, and the fact that every (it seemed to her) black man in Hollywood or pro sports married a white woman, Cora figured there would just be one white man who dated one black woman in every ten thousand biracial couples. So out of 100,000 white men, only 10 would date black women, and out of those ten, nine would not be serious enough to take their black woman to the altar. Cora had no idea how she came up with those statistics, but she was sure they were right. Maybe that white man dated that black woman as a way of going against what his parents had preached, satisfying his own curiosity, challenging his homosexual tendencies, or trying to prove to himself that he could have a mind of his own. She also thought that white men, if they dated a black woman at all, looked for someone with substance; a title, a profession, a high profile. Black men were apparently not so picky. Cora didn't think that her theory on this issue was a far-fetched one, although she knew that the black men who had made that choice would not agree; in fact would be quite pissed off at the notion. It also made perfect sense to Cora that a white innately homosexual, but somewhat homophobic male, would be more comfortable trying to be heterosexual with a black woman before venturing into full-fledged heterosexuality; or for that matter, deciding to come out of the closet. She, the black woman, would be a tryout of sorts, a stepping stone. Cora thought that there were lots of men who were by nature gay, who didn't really want to be gay, for whatever reason, and wanted to try being straight. Didn't nurses practice sticking hypodermic needles into oranges before feeling confident enough to 'attack' a human arm? It was pretty much the same thing, in Cora's thinking, and she was pretty darn sure she was right. Hell, yeah! In relationships such as these, the woman could mistake it for love. Worse than her mistake, would be his. *He* could also mistake it for love; but in time he would fall back on what he'd been taught; know that in the long run he would need a white woman to bear his children so they wouldn't have to strangle their own souls when society had a go at them, and made their blackness and mixed race identity oppression-worthy. She would see his occasional embarrassment, his seeking to disassociate with her in certain situations. He would act as though nothing had happened once they were back at home. She would interpret the experience as just what it was—embarrassment and disassociation. She would keep her cool; take her mind off it. She would refuse to stare that demon of racism and rejection in the face because it frightened her.

Son of a bitch!

Maybe that's why Charlie was pure white. Cora's mind was beginning to formulate more statistics. Charlie must have been the offspring of the white wife his father took when he exited the life of his black woman, whoever she was. Or, maybe, Charlie's dad had never strayed out of his race, had not had culturally diverse experiences, which meant he had only mingled with white women. Was it then, just Charlie's bright idea to get up close and personal with all the varieties of his species? After all, they were all right here in America, sitting in his high school classes, attending the same parties, the same sporting events. All these thoughts were dancing around in Cora's head and making it throb. As usual, she was thinking too much; analyzing everything; trying to read each detail of her daughter's life as a sign of some impending trouble that the girl had to be protected from. Cora's own stinging memories of her years with Mike lingered in her heart like the taste of rhubarb on the tongue. A mother sees herself in her daughter, reads her eyes, accurately interprets every half smile, every sigh, every flare of the nostril, every sway of the hip. She just knew that Julia was headed for trouble with that relationship. What form that trouble would take and how soon it would come, Cora didn't yet know. Was Julia following her mother's path through that valley of self-esteem death? It was a death from which Cora had now come back, but not without a struggle and the fiercest determination to be alive, emotionally healthy, and once again in full possession of herself. She would not live like grass in New Jersey—pretty much taken for granted, a victim of the lawn mower's blade that would, in summer, make her plain and flat and even for feet to walk on; nor would she be left to grow unnoticed like grass in Brooklyn, overrun by weeds, hardened and brown from neglect. Rather, she would live like a beautiful, exotic tree, maybe a tropically cultured bush, carefully manicured into a pampered poodle, or lush green pom-pom.

As that wild idea of being a sculpted bush played across Cora's mind, a smile formed at the corners of her mouth. She was now considering herself topiary. She liked that she could always find a way to laugh at herself. She took a deep breath, pursed her lips, and decided to keep her thoughts about the relationship between Charlie and Julia to herself—at least for now. She knew that all seemed well, but she was more experienced and had actually lived the old adage: *All that glitters is not gold.*

Each of Cora's experiences as part of an interracial couple had made a hole somewhere in her heart. Some holes were small, some holes were medium, and some holes were extremely large. There was a giant-sized hole that Mike had made one day—unknown to himself, perhaps, but acutely felt by Cora. In this large hole nestled her biggest fear that one day these holes in her heart would become so many and so close together that there'd be less and less tissue connecting them. She greatly feared that these little threads of tissue would eventually disappear altogether, and she would end up with one big, vacant space where her heart used to be. There was nothing more frightening to Cora than the thought of losing herself, and she knew that it was happening, slowly but surely. When she first met Michael she was a sophisticated, classy, calm and confident person; in fact these were the very qualities that had attracted him to her. As time went by, however, she found that she was full of self-doubt, and felt generally uneasy in her skin. About seven months into the relationship, she had discussed her feelings with him, and he had reassured her that he loved her, and that they should probably just spend more time together. He seemed genuine enough at the time. It was a conversation they had had on New Year's Eve. Cora had picked New Year's Eve because she always thought it was a good time to end old things and start new ones, or at least get rid of problematic, unhealthy situations. Mike had seemed open-minded enough, and she communicated to him that she was sure he loved her, but could only tell him how he made her feel, and it was not a good feeling. If only she had gone with her gut!

A subsequent experience of Cora's in another interracial relationship with someone named Ken, also ended up down the tubes, but it hadn't brought her the misery that the former relationship had; it had really just been a very strange experience; one she recalled intermittently and only for a few seconds at a time, mostly with a feeling of total neutrality. Mostly.

Chapter 2

Julia: "Girls just want to have fun."

Boys, and the possibility of fleshy entanglements with boys, were the only thoughts on Julia's mind these days. She loved the sultry summer nights when the genders mingled and engaged not in carefree activity and idle chatter, but in obviously lustful interaction, forbidden sexual intercourse, or at least heavy petting that could fog up a car window faster than a blast of arctic air in January. Julia felt ready to be an active participant in these things, but her upbringing was strict, and she felt that she was always under her mother's watchful eye, which indeed she was. In Cora's mind, Julia wasn't ready for anything. To the contrary, she thought that Julia was still her little girl, and the mantra where her daughter's interaction with boys was concerned was always, "Hold it, young lady, not so fast."

The late June evening was pregnant with just that kind of sexy business waiting to go full throttle at nightfall. It would intensify as teenagers gathered together and adults sought to unwind after a long day of work. Men would stroll the beach with or without partners. Women on the lookout for a man's attention would walk their dogs in clogs and short shorts; teenage boys in cars, windows down, would be fooling around, blasting their music; teenage couples sat in convertibles hugging and kissing. The boldest of the girls who were about Julia's age would give up their virginity under blankets near the bluff.

Julia sat on a low, wide rock and let her toes touch the edge of the water. However, what she felt was not the coolness of the water on her feet, but the dampness in her crotch as she thought about her boyfriend, Charlie. Earlier today, he had suddenly stopped during their lazy stroll in the park, leaned her up against the trunk of a large tree, and pressed his hardness against her as he sought her lips, at the same time making that slightly up-and-down, slightly circular motion between her legs. Now, there was that dampness and familiar sweetness between her legs again.

Many girls at school had vied for Charlie's attention, but Julia had been the lucky one. He didn't originally cross her mind as a potential beau though she had seen his looks of admiration when she passed him in the halls. Julia knew that she possessed the exotic looks that came with being of mixed race, but didn't think Charlie had any reason to be attracted to her. She watched pushier types go after him tooth and nail, and was sure that one of them would, sooner rather than later, put her hooks in him and claim him as her own. She was completely taken by surprise when he asked her to accompany him to his hockey team's fundraiser. She knew it was a well-attended, very elegant affair. The parents came out in droves, and the competition they staged among themselves was fierce. The mothers tried to out-dress each other, and the fathers amplified their positions at work in an effort to make the best impression, or be the envy of the others. The only teenagers in attendance were the hockey team's members and the girls they had invited as dates. Parents kept an eye out to see whom their daughters and sons were attached to, and judged the youngsters by their parents' apparent socio-economic status. Were their folks new in their companies and firms trying to get a foothold on rung one of the corporate ladder; were they sure-footed in a quickly upward climb, or already established and sitting comfortably at the top? Did the husband's accomplishments manifest in the designer choice of his wife's dress and or the cost of her jewelry? Was she a working wife, (*a.k.a.* Poor Thing), or a lady who lunched? And exactly what car did they have valet-parked tonight? A Benz? Beamer, Lexus, Infiniti, Hummer, maybe? It had better not be a Hyundai anything, although that Sonata could be mistaken for a Jaguar in the dark. Miss the slanted *H*, and you've been had. Cheap cars were looking better and better these days. Price-conscious folks or those who were mindful of the ever-disappearing greenness of the planet could be tempted to drive one of those things to a function, no matter how elegant, but warning: If a cheap car was anywhere in the vicinity of this event, then that couple would be well advised to come late and leave early, so no one would be any the wiser about what they were driving.

Julia knew it was the kind of event that her mother, Cora, would really not care to attend. Neither would Cora's man, Clayton Sax. Julia was proud of the fact that her mother was a woman very much in charge of herself, and very clear about not having to keep up with the Joneses. Actually, she wasn't even quite sure who the Joneses were most of the time. She possessed herself, and lived by her own standards. Those who knew her well admired those qualities in her. Such was Julia's thinking as she debated whether or not to accept Charlie's invitation. To her, these big events were neither here nor there; she could just as well pass on this one. However, if Cora wasn't going to be attending, maybe she should go and be with her peers un-chaperoned for a change. For Julia, deciding to go out usually boiled down to how she felt on the day or night of the event, but this was different. Tickets had to be purchased well in advance. Julia thought these thoughts with a certain degree of disdain for those parents whom she considered fickle-minded, but knew that this was real life in their world. She had seen these people show up in school to handle matters related to their children. They came in with a flourish and as much fanfare as possible—whatever fanfare it was possible to muster up as they sought to get past the security guard at the front desk. Security guards in schools, as everyone knows, have the clear and singular goal of belittling the people who need their permission to get into the school. They are especially rude to those who come in well dressed and a little uppity. You could almost see them thinking, "Your threads and bling don't impress me, B....! And is that your fab ride directly across the street? Watching it ain't my job, B....!" and after chucking the sign-in book in Mr. or Mrs. Uppity's direction and swinging the attached pen around by its chain, they walk a few steps away from the desk, and with their hands in their pockets and a scornful glare at the now Mr. or Mrs. Reduced-To-Poor-Slob, silently dare him or her to ask one more question.

Mr. or Mrs. Reduced-To-Poor-Slob would scribble quickly in the book and begin to drift down the hallway, taking three or four steps in one direction, stopping abruptly and beginning to go in the opposite direction. It would be a big relief if a student happened by and came to the rescue with directions.

Julia herself drove a nifty little teal blue convertible Lexus, given to her by her mother for her sixteenth birthday, not because Cora thought her daughter needed to make an impression at school, but because the girl liked the car, and her mother always got her what she wanted. Julia thoroughly enjoyed driving it, and was glad not to have a handed down station wagon. There were kids who actually had to get up the courage to drive these things to school. She chuckled to herself, not with any feeling of superiority. She just thought those cars were funny-looking, the way their front protruded and their back suddenly squared off. She had the same quirky sense of humor that Cora possessed, and could just as easily be amused by her own thoughts as by any comedian in the high school auditorium, or the local pub.

She decided to accept Charlie's invitation to the event without too much thought about what it meant or what he wanted, or for that matter, what *she* herself wanted. She could wear her gold BCBG Max Azria heels from last summer. She had worn them only once. She would have Cora help her pick out a new dress, and she could go with one of her friends for hair and nails on the day of the event. She hoped that her mother would let her buy something sexy; not whorish, just very glam and sexy enough to make her feel that way.

By the time Charlie picked Julia up that night for their date at the fundraiser, she had decided that she was going out with him basically because he had asked. She was a girl, it might be fun, and after all, girls just want to have fun. Cindy Lauper had said so way back when. She remembered seeing the singer on the Johnny Carson Show once when she was watching TV with Cora. She was much younger then, but she remembered that. She remembered because it was way past her bedtime, but for some reason she could not remember now, Cora had allowed her to stay up.

That night, after the dinner-dance, Charlie asked Julia to become his steady girlfriend and she agreed. Her heart was not in it at the time, but she didn't think any harm could come of saying yes to a guy like Charlie. He was popular at school, an excellent hockey player, and he was desired and overtly chased by many girls at school. In addition, he was smart and well-mannered, financially well-off and noticeably handsome. What's not to like?

Chapter 3

Ken: "I'll do as I darned well please."

Ken Rudolph had taken a job as chef aboard *The Big Payoff* after leaving his parents' house in Wisconsin in a huff early one morning. On the previous night, he had had a major argument with his father who thought that his son should be taking over the family business. The cattle raising business was a good one, and had made the Rudolphs quite a fortune. Now Gus Rudolph was aging and wanted to pass the business on to his only son, in fact, his only child, but Ken was not the least bit interested in that venture. He loved food, wine, and sailing. Even as a child he had been fascinated with the cooking shows on television, and would browse through all the recipe books and wine magazines he could find at the local Barnes and Noble bookstore. After the relationship between him and Cora Jenkins dissolved, he became a restaurateur with financial backing from his parents. It was not what they wanted him to do, but they figured he was a young man who would learn from his mistakes and come to his senses.

Well, lately Ken's restaurant business had been in a slump. His next move was what he was attempting to discuss with his father that last night they were together, but the senior Rudolph was showing neither empathy nor understanding. He told his son that his restaurant idea had been a dumb one from the start, and was bound to end the way it was doing now.

"That's what happens when children are above the sound advice of their parents," Gus Rudolph told his son.

In a tone that betrayed his annoyance and aggravation with the older man's attitude, Ken reminded his father that he had always made it clear to his family that he had no interest in cows, nor the milk and beef they were good for. The cheeses he needed to go along with his wine, he could buy at gourmet shops, but they hadn't taken him seriously. In the usual fashion of parents, they had ignored him and figured that he would eventually come around to their way of thinking. At forty seven, they still thought it wasn't too late for their son to learn some sense.

As his father spoke, it dawned on Ken that his parents would not get it if they lived to be two hundred years, and where these things were concerned, his parents shared a brain, anyway; something he was aware of even in his childhood. Ken argued his point vehemently, and expressed to his father his disdain for the older man's attempt at controlling everything and everyone around him.

That morning, Ken kissed his mother goodbye and left the house vowing to cut the parental ties once and for all and live his dreams. There had to be some merit to the words he had once heard her say to his dad when he tried to tell her what to do about something that was clearly not his business to butt into. Ken reflected now that only last night, Mr. Rudolph had been explaining to Mrs. Rudolph why he preferred a different haircut on her. He couldn't remember now, what his mother's exact defense of her choice had been, so he put the thought out of his mind. He did, however, recall hearing his mother say to her husband about other interferences in the past, "I'll do as I darned well please." Not that she had ever had the courage to put those words into practice in all those years of marriage, but she had said them. Ken frowned and exhaled hard as he wondered what would make a woman give her power over to a man. His mother was a smart and beautiful woman, but somehow, around Gus Rudolph she seemed to own very little of her self. Well, that was *her* problem, he finalized in his mind as he stormed out of the house and closed the door behind him. In his soul he hoped he'd have the resolve to stay away from the two of them forever now.

He had always felt the lure of the ocean even though childhood had not afforded Ken much experience with it. This was his big chance to be totally involved with food, wine, and sailing; to have his heart's interests combined into one great lifestyle. He didn't need to fuss over patrons, organize waiters, supervise catering and decorating for special events, smile at food critics, *or* sit with a CPA reconciling accounts. He would cook, drink, and sail. That was his plan and he was sticking to it. As luck would have it, Ken quickly found a ship on which to sail away to his happiness. At first he couldn't believe his own luck, but then he remembered that a few years earlier he had read a book called *The Secret*, and had since then made a point of keeping his desires as the consistent focus of his thinking so that his heart's yearnings would show up as his life; the life he dreamed of.

"That's it." Ken heard himself say. "It isn't luck at all. It's the impartial, unbending law of the universe."

He felt good knowing that there was at least this one big thing about his life that his folks could not tamper with: his thoughts and their manifestation as his reality. This was the one big thing that he was totally in charge of. How cool was that!

The young Rudolph enjoyed his new life cooking and drifting on the ocean from port to port. He thought that life on this yacht was first class.

He put himself in charge of preparing all the meals on the very first day he was on board the ship. No one seemed to mind. In his galley kitchen he always kept rare condiments and spices, a variety of sauces that he had concocted himself, and wines that he collected from various countries. There was always an ample supply of Champagne, specifically Louis Roederer Cristal, and Veuve Clicquot Demi Sec—these he considered a staple for long cruises. He insisted on using only the best ingredients for the incredible dishes he made and named after his own experiences of fun and adventure. He was the creator of Aspen Chicken, and Filet Mignon de Nuit Parisien. If he ever served something as ordinary as pan-seared swordfish, he would be sure to add some exotic spices and name it something else. He wore the biggest grin as he served these dishes to his shipmates and explained how they got their names. It was not unusual to have three or four stories related to one entrée. Ken never *did* care about rations and portions, and the guests who sometimes came aboard to visit the crew or at the captain's invitation, didn't seem to, either. Great food was great food and the more one had of it the merrier. There *was* plenty of food, and Ken wanted to serve it to his guests himself so he could share the story or the origin of each dish. In one short month on board the ship, he had come to know well enough, though not intimately, the other two men on his ship, Gilbert and Clarence, and was able to live comfortably with them. There was also a woman on board, Thelma. To him, life on that ship was indeed La Dolce Vita.

Ken Rudolph actually looked very young for forty seven. Life so far had been good to him. He was well-read and widely traveled and had even had a stint in France, training at one of Paris's finest cooking schools. In fact, it was at the Louvre in Paris, eighteen years earlier, that he had first encountered Cora Jenkins. He had been standing outside in the morning air admiring the modern pyramid that stood in front of the museum, and smiling as he thought of the throng of people he'd seen inside, pressed together in their effort to get a snapshot of the Mona Lisa. It was then that Cora sauntered by between the sculpture and him. Her voluptuous bosom, small waist, and curvy hips had created a sensuous profile, and he let his eyes follow her for several seconds. Later, they would share a bench at the Champs Elysees, and decide to do their sightseeing together over the next few days. They usually met at noon as the day was gradually warming. Summers in Paris were inclined to begin their mornings on the cool side, and turn pleasantly warm by mid-day. It was Ken's last week in that beautiful city, and Cora's two-week vacation there was winding down, too. She had gone to France to get over her breakup with Mike. France, somehow, had always been very comfortable and comforting to her. It was there that she cooled out for long weekends during her college days in England. During her six-year romance with Mike, she had made several more trips there, and had discovered Sacre Coeur and Moulin Rouge and a whole slew of fine, new restaurants and shopping plazas. Now it seemed the natural choice for just getting away. Her thirtieth birthday was coming; too soon she thought; in two years, but too soon. She knew she needed time to heal her heart. She would enter the thirties feeling whole. A romantic liaison had been nowhere in her plans. The little tours with Ken initially had about the same degree of excitement as meeting a girlfriend for lunch. She was happy to meet up with him, but not particularly thrilled. There was no sexual tension, as it's called, and certainly no butterflies in her stomach. She ducked into her sweater, pulled on her jeans, and slid into her mules, making no special effort to appear physically attractive to him.

By the time Ken and Cora got back to the United States, however, they had established a very close, albeit ambivalent relationship. She couldn't exactly call him her man, but they were definitely more than friends. Cora noticed that there was always a relaxed air about Ken that made him look like he had just come back from a day at the spa. She liked that. She knew that she enjoyed, without lusting, the fresh look and smell of him. She felt that they could be friends forever. Fourteen months later, though, the two were to go their separate ways and live apart with not so much as a greeting card at Christmas, or a birthday remembered.

Chapter 4

Clarence: "The universe is beautiful and kind."

Sailing leisurely on *The Big Payoff*, Clarence Morley stood at the helm of the ship, and soaked in the serenity of the blueness above and below him. This new job let him stay on the bridge alone for as long as he wanted, sometimes fourteen hours at a time; not a long time to him. He thought the silence afforded by the absence of human voices was a very special kind of luxury, and he deeply appreciated the vast open sky and silvery luminescence of the ocean. Neither the sky nor the sea looked the same on any two days, or for that matter, in any two hours. He never tired of gazing at them. The ship just about sailed itself, and he got to read or think of nothing in particular most of the time, which was his own kind of meditative practice.

Clarence was recently retired from strategic air command in the armed forces, and could live without the constant hustle and bustle and the major responsibilities he had in that position. Though he really loved his job while it lasted, it was something that caused him quite a bit of stress. Now he thoroughly enjoyed not having to deal with people up close. As long as daily life was at an even pace, he had no desire to ask any questions or engage in the idle chatter so common among co-workers. Cheffy, as Ken was sometimes fondly called by some of the crew, though never by Clarence, cooked him his midday and evening meals and relieved him for about five or six hours every day so he could get some sleep. Occasionally the two exchanged a nod or a half-smile. That was the extent of their pleasantries. Each considered the relationship between them decent enough and workable. What either man knew about the private or previous life of the other, neither knew, and that was fine by both.

One of the reasons Clarence didn't speak much to anyone about anyone was that he had no one to speak about. He had no family of his own, and the members of his original nuclear family were dead. His parents had died when he was still a young boy, maybe nine, and he was raised by a busy surgeon of an uncle; a single man. So at an early age, Clarence learned to spend time alone and be happy doing so. This only uncle died of prostate cancer when Clarence was fourteen. From then on, the youngster pretty much raised himself, and had grown accustomed to his own company. He read many books on spirituality, understood that souls chose their circumstances and the bodies they would enter long before birth, and knew that everything in the world was just the way it ought to be. He read the Desiderata daily, and tried to live by all its tenets. With this heightened level of spiritual awareness and his knowing that he was an inalienable child of the universe fully ingrained in his mind and being, Clarence found it unnecessary to seek people out for their friendship or companionship. As far as he was concerned, his soul had chosen this aloneness before birth as a way of aiding its own evolution, and he had humbly accepted the conditions. He accepted anyone who entered into his life, but was careful to maintain enough distance between them and himself so as not to confuse their beliefs and convictions with his own. He also graciously let them leave his life when that time came. Of all the authors he had read who delved into spirituality and matters of the soul, he had become particularly fond of Gary Zukov, and kept a book of his quotes on his nightstand. From time to time he would pick out a quote, and ponder it for several days, making sure to fully glean its meaning and figure out some application of it to his own life, before moving on to a new one. On his person he kept photos of his parents and uncle now gone to their rest. The small photographs were layered in a silver locket that he kept in his pocket; and so Clarence thought himself always somehow connected to a world of loving spirits, known and unknown. He was very comfortable with the relationship he had established with his shipmates. They respected him, and for the most part, let him be. He had once had a conversation with Thelma, the secretary/housekeeper on board the ship, for three minutes. He knew it was three minutes because she had walked into the kitchen just as he dropped an egg into a small pot of water on the stove, and removed it just about the time the egg timer was going off and she was saying goodbye. He always had a three-minute egg for breakfast with one cup of sugarless, black coffee (Total carbohydrates first thing in the morning: Zero). Up to that point, it was the longest he had spoken to any member of that crew, and as far as he was concerned, that was long enough. His colleagues were all well aware, though, that no bad blood existed between them and him. His distant manner was purely a matter of personality. They had all agreed that there was something not just quiet, but very serene, almost sacred about Clarence, and when he was present in a space everything and everyone around him took on an unexplainable aura of calm. He was also strikingly handsome, which added to the wonder of him.

Clarence hadn't originally planned to work on *The Big Payoff*. He had just been, as the song says, sitting on the dock of the bay, wasting time. It had only been a few days after he retired from his military post, when

Gilbert Jacobs came along, about to board the ship which Clarence had been watching gently bobbing up and down in the little harbor where it was anchored.

"Going Somewhere? Gilbert had asked casually.

"No. Just sitting here," Clarence replied without looking up.

"Want to come with?" was Gilbert's next question.

"Why not?" Clarence replied with no thought or hesitation.

And with that, he followed Gilbert up the plank, onto the boat. He had acquired some sailing skills along the route of his life which Gilbert gladly put to use. They were happy with each other although they didn't talk much, and Clarence never saw a reason to leave. Every day that he looked at the open sky and the tremendous ocean bathed in shades of blue and green and silvery gray, he considered himself a lucky man because he had had no plans for his life prior to being invited on board that vessel. Now he had a job that he enjoyed and got to spend as much time alone as he desired. His present circumstances confirmed his belief that if one took the path of least resistance, life would unfold itself and present precious gifts, which one had only to accept. With a grateful heart, Clarence said out loud every morning as he got out of bed, "The universe is beautiful and kind."

Chapter 5

Thelma: "Still waters run deep."

There were only four people who permanently lived on board *The Big Payoff* now. One of them was Thelma who was basically the housekeeper and secretary; a woman of very, *very* few words. She hadn't always been that way. In her youth, she had been quite a pistol, gorgeous and fun-loving like most people in the prime of their lives, but her life's experiences had rendered her cynical and bitter. Now, she trusted no one. She believed none of what she heard, and only half of what she saw, as some would put it.

When Thelma accepted the job on the boat, she hoped that the ocean in its abundance of water would drown her sorrow; that her bitter memories would go out with an ebbing tide; but that hadn't happened. She knew it would be difficult, with Gilbert's presence a constant and daily reminder of how she got there in the first place, but she hoped for the best. All these years later, her pain was dull but always present; her desire for revenge in a light sleep; dormant, but by no means dead.

Now in her late sixties, she still carried herself with an upright, elegant posture, and you could tell that she had once been a woman of class and very good looks although a smile never crossed her face. When there was a party on board, she was given the role of waitress. She served the guests in a robot-like manner keeping her eyes fixed on the tray from which they daintily picked up their food, so mostly she just saw people's hands—a sort of curiosity if you considered their various shapes, and sizes, and degrees of manicure. Thelma, like Clarence, enjoyed the solitude of her life at sea. When she wasn't serving guests she made schedules and notes as directed by the captain, Gilbert. She took her orders without asking questions, did what she had to do, and retired to her cabin. What she did in her cabin, only *she* knew.

To those who knew Thelma, she always seemed calm and emotionless. She was never one to get into a fluster or frenzy over anything or anyone. On that boat, she had seen celebrities come and go at those elaborate parties which Gilbert loved to throw. She never gushed over them, she never tried to get an autograph, she didn't even really care who they were. She might have mistaken Morgan for Denzel, and Julia for Angelina; Tom Pitt, Brad Cruise; who knew? They were all handsome people with too much time and money, if anyone asked her. In Thelma's opinion, it was an uneven distribution of wealth and good looks. Add egoism, fame, and an awestruck, star-struck public to the equation and you were bound to have trouble. No wonder they were professing their love for their spouses one week, and having a bitter divorce the next. They also checked in and out of rehab like nobody's business. Celebrities were all the same to her; people moving around in the background scenery of real life. In essence she agreed with William Shakespeare that all of life was some sort of stage, and all its men and women merely playing around until it came time for their exits and their entrances. She watched their performances from a distance, and without physical or emotional intrusion into their world.

The people who came in contact with Thelma considered her to be conservative, maybe even a little removed from life. No emotion was given away by a frown at her brow, or a smile on her lips. The color of her skin was deep and rich; its texture smooth. It made one think of chocolate porcelain, and her facial expression was as tight as the bun in her hair; not tight with a tension or obvious worry, just pulled together tight; like expressionless. No one who met Thelma had any clue how turbulent her mind actually was, how much she hated one particular member of her crew, how many times she woke up in a panic in the middle of the night and rushed to the bathroom sink to wash off the blood that was all over her hands from just having slit his throat. On her worst nights, that same dream would recur two or three times. Each time, she would wake up and dash to the sink, see that her hands were dry and clean, return to bed, and start the dream all over again. None of this internal chaos was displayed to the people Thelma interacted with daily, or occasionally. Her demeanor was bland and stoic, but like the sages say, and as any old lady on your block would tell you: "Still waters run deep."

Chapter 6

Gilbert: "Let the good times roll."

Last, but mightiest of them all, was the boss and captain; a man in his late sixties named Gilbert Jacobs. He owned the ship. It had been a birthday gift to himself on his sixtieth birthday. The dream he had as a young man when he graduated high school had been fully realized. By the time he was forty-five, he had made an obscene amount of money in real estate, and would never have to work another day in his life. It seemed that Gilbert had been born to do just what he was doing—sailing the open seas, living well, having his choice of land or ocean living. For most of the year, though, he chose the ocean. Especially now that his children were older and virtually out of his life, he had precious little reason to be stuck where someone could reach him on a land line that was listed in a phone book, or worse, happen to be in his neighborhood and come knocking on his door to pay an unexpected visit.

Confident, filthy rich, flamboyant, and graying slightly at the temples, he had a sophisticated look and a wry smile that seemed to say he had an ace up his sleeve. He loved traveling with this small crew. In a way, they had become his family. Several times a year he would throw a lavish party on the ship, usually when he was around the west coast of the United States. He would dock the ship and have a get-together on board for some of the most important names in Hollywood. Of course, several directors and stars would be invited. There was easily a score or more of this party clan to be found in and around the place at any time of the year, except for a few of them who might have been away, either shooting a movie or promoting one. No big deal. Gilbert's guests were always allowed to bring someone along, so his parties never lacked a full compliment of friends. They would show up to chitchat and schmooze and lobby for the roles they wanted to have, or thought they were born to play. It would all be done under the guise and pretense of just being out with friends for another night of luxurious fun, but indeed, that yacht became a casting couch of sorts for those in that industry, used to buying and selling favors whenever they had an opportunity to do so.

Gilbert had a single agenda at these parties. His job was to create a festive occasion that gathered people together; and although he was as charming as a prince to the beautiful or famous (sometimes both beautiful and famous) women who showed up on his ship for these festivities, he didn't wish to bed a single one of them. He didn't have a role to offer them, anyway, and he knew that was the one thing for which they would exchange their favors. These types were hoping for introductions to the 'right' people, although most of them were pushy enough to introduce themselves, or had an agent. So Gilbert Jacobs knew that his role was to provide the party spot, the food, and the liquor, gather the people together, and just let the good times roll. He wanted each party to top the previous one, and he went all out to achieve that.

With two marriages behind him, Gilbert had now settled into a single and luxurious lifestyle, and was determined to enjoy it thoroughly. He had one son born to him from each marriage; Brock by his first wife and

Charlie by his second, but he didn't see much of either of the boys, and never saw their mothers at all. He had instead, over the years, accumulated a number of high profile friends whose company he enjoyed. They, in turn, enjoyed time spent on his boat and admired his penchant for the lavish lifestyle. They considered him to be cut from the same cloth as they were, just not in pictures. If there was a good time to be had, it would be wherever and whenever Gilbert was throwing a party.

Thelma's presence on Gilbert's ship should have cramped the captain's style, but it didn't. Gilbert considered what transpired between him and Thelma all those years ago, "just one of those things." As far as he was concerned, he had made it up to her and felt no guilt or remorse; he had moved on. He figured that Thelma had moved on also, and so he didn't consider her presence on his ship a hindrance to his lifestyle, let alone a threat to his life.

Book 2

Chapter 1

Cora's own marriage situation, or lack of one, was a big pain in the behind, apart from that interracial situation with Charlie and her daughter, Julia. At 46, Cora thought she would have been married and settled, and celebrating a significant anniversary, but she was still a single woman. She was self-sufficient and attractive, but very single. Not that a man had never proposed marriage to her; she had just somehow thought that he wasn't quite the one, and had held out for Mr. Right. She thought she should feel some kind of magic in his presence; some kind of light-headedness; some eagerness to own his love and soul. So far, no one had really done that for her, well not since Mike. Her present relationship with Clayton Sax was solid and safe; almost too much so, but she just didn't feel like marrying him.

Clayton and Cora returned from Faustine's, a nice little pub in Cora's neighborhood that the two popped into from time to time. This evening, they stopped in after a leisurely browse through the local art gallery where an unknown artist was featuring his watercolor works. It was someone they had never heard of, but it didn't matter. Going to the gallery this evening was just something they could do together. Now they wanted a drink before going home, and this was one of the little spots close to home that Cora loved going to. The two walked hand in hand through the streets. The summer air seemed to kiss their cheeks, and Clayton was thinking there was no way he could live without Cora at his side. They stopped at the fancy little joint which featured a pianist each night, and seated only forty or fifty people. The place actually felt more like a private lounge than a neighborhood pub, with its softly pleated, dark red velvet drapes hanging against glossy chocolate walls. There were elaborate sparkling chandeliers dangling languidly from the ceiling, and luxurious Baktiari rugs were seemingly carelessly strewn all over the hickory suede floor.

The couple sat next to each other at a small round table, and Clayton ordered a dry martini that he figured would quickly take the edge off his nerves. Cora ordered her usual Scotch and ginger ale. She liked that mix. Adding ginger ale made it not exactly hard liquor, but strong enough to let her relax. In social settings, it peeled back just enough of her inhibitions to allow her to have a good time. It let her talk to strangers and smile widely. It also let her dance unrepressed—with a certain degree of abandon that onlookers, male and female, found sexy and attractive.

In the middle of their museum stroll, Clayton had asked Cora to marry him. This was the third time he had asked her to marry him, and the third time she had declined, citing "unreadiness for the level of commitment necessary for such a union." Her daughter still lived at home, Cora went on to explain and she didn't want to push her out. At this point in her life, living with a man would have to be a beautifully carved out life for two, and only two. Cora was officially done with her child rearing years, but wanted to give her daughter the time she needed to decide to move out and do so, unhurried. Julia had hinted that she might want to go out of state to college, anyway. That would be in about another year. Cora wasn't spending her time with anyone else, that wasn't it. In fact, she liked Clayton quite a bit. They called each other several times a day and she did not make any important decisions without talking to him about them. They shared a lot of each other's lives. Their lovemaking was open and unfettered. It was as close to perfect love as one could get, yet she was reluctant to be hitched. For one thing, she wasn't changing her name, and she wasn't explaining to anyone who might be wondering if they were married that yes, they were, but she'd decided to keep her own name. Keeping the maiden name was not that unusual in some circles, but black women always took their husband's name, and proudly flaunted their **MRS**. status. Cora thought that the only black women who could keep their own name and not be questioned about it, were people who had made a name for themselves in the world, and whom everyone had come to know by their first and maiden names like Goldie Hawn, or for that matter, by their first names only, like Oprah. Clayton's mother had been Mrs. Clayton Sax II. Clayton thought Mrs. Clayton Sax III would be nice for Cora, but she had not been willing to acquiesce. In a strange and unexplainable way she felt that changing her last name, especially at this late stage in her life, would take away from the woman she essentially was. One should only be made to do this name-changing thing if one was very young and planned to have a family whose members should all have the same last name, or.... if one had to go into a witness protection program, Cora was thinking with that quirky side of her brain.

Clayton had been raised on as good a side of the tracks as Cora was, and was her social equal. He had become a hotshot corporate executive at IBM, made a six-figure income in addition to handsome bonuses, and had an affluent lifestyle. The two had traveled together on several of Clayton's business trips that had him jetting back and forth between New York and L.A, and sometimes as far away as Paris or Stockholm, but he wasn't offering Cora anything novel—except you wanted to consider the fact that he was the first black man she had had any kind of serious, long-term relationship with. He knew that she was comfortable with him. She had told him so. She had commented on the fact that being out with him was easy since they didn't draw any attention to themselves as a couple. She felt that he was always in her corner, so to speak. There was no way society could accept or reject one without the other, an experience she had become accustomed to, first with Mike and later with Ken, so there was that element of comfort in the relationship with Clayton. When they argued, which rarely was the case, she never struggled to interpret the look in his eyes. It was pain or anger pure and simple. There was never a question in her mind that there could be anything else. When he made love to her, there was no hint of reservation and no attempt at brushing hair away from her face. She had seen her white boyfriend make that sweeping movement with his hand across her face, even though she wore a short hairstyle at the time, and wondered what the hell he was seeing. He seemed to be moving imaginary tresses of maybe blond hair away from her face. She was curious about his fantasies while making love to her, but she never shared her thoughts with him, or dared ask the question. Cora now recalled a time when she had decided to repaint her deck herself for the sake of having a project. Mike, her beau at the time, had volunteered to help and she had let him. They chatted light heartedly as they painted and all was going well, but in one of those instances when he bent over to fill his brush, he came up to hit her square in the face and got white paint on her forehead. She had interpreted it as his subconscious wish that she was white, and told him so. They both laughed nervously about it, and there was not a denial on his part that this was his thinking. What lawyers say about silence in the face of adverse accusation being an admission of guilt now struck Cora as something else she should have taken more seriously. Later that day, he explained why he hadn't yet asked her to meet his parents although he had been seeing her for three years by then. His brother Hal had greatly upset their parents by dating a woman who was separated from her husband, but not divorced. This had earned him the title of *the bad son*. If he, *"the good son"* were now to bring a black woman home, his brother's sin would pale by comparison. Maybe he could take a chance with telling his father, who was less educated but much more liberal minded, but he definitely could not tell his mother. *She* could never handle it, and her heart was already in such bad shape from complications of diabetes. He'd better just leave well enough alone. And what would his mother's friends think? She would certainly now appear less in their eyes. He was the son she had always bragged about, her little one; the good one. Recently, Disney had accepted some lyrics he wrote for use in one of their upcoming projects, and he had added another feather to mom's proverbial cap. He couldn't disappoint her. His dead grandmother would turn over in her grave if he dared bring a schwartze home. As a child, Mike had been driven through black neighborhoods with his mother and grandmother, and they had made sure to point out where the schwartzes lived, adding as many derogatory statements about that group as they could manage to think of. Cora had seen the inherited attitudes reflected in Mike's behavior from time to time. As they watched a TV program in a hotel room one day, one which featured a black woman as the design director of the Ford Motor Company, Mike was openly cynical, if not disdainful, and made comments that had the equivalent sentiment of a school boy's colloquial: "Yeah, Right!" It was his disbelief that anyone of that group could have a job of such importance; maybe it was one of those affirmative action deals. In her usual calm manner, Cora asked Mike if he had any white paint left for this woman. He turned to her and said, "About the other day, better than you I know I'll never find. The only problem with you is your complexion. Cora wondered if Mike had plans to leave the country now that the U.S. had elected a black president.

Cora wondered about something else, too. She wondered if Mike could be spared from her latent wrath, which she knew would eventually come to the surface. After all, she had moved on. She didn't understand how love for one man and hatred for another could nestle side-by-side like Siamese twins in the same bosom; but they did.

Mike's being ashamed of her had become a giant hole in Cora's heart unknown to him. He had made it clear, purposely or not, that she was only good enough for a clandestine liaison with him. He could only woo her behind turned backs and eyes that were watching elsewhere; and although she knew that *he* was the one guilty of the sin of ultimate hypocrisy, she felt ashamed. Something about the secrecy that surrounded the relationship brought to mind the stories of house slaves whose masters secretly slept with them unknown to their families. They would do the deed out somewhere in the fields, and at the end of it the women would quietly return to their chores of serving lunch, or caring for his children as though nothing had happened. He would return to the role of master, haughty and aloof.

Such were the stories and thoughts that Cora shared freely with Clayton, never wondering if he would judge her, consider himself her last choice, or think that she was with him because her other relationships had not been successful. They had that kind of easy and supportive friendship. In Clayton's workplace he held up standards of excellence to be met by colleagues and subordinates, and he made no compromises there, but with those he loved there was total acceptance. There were no queries, no requests for changes, upgrades, improvements, or newness. He had been seeing Cora for three years, and for three years his love for her had been unwavering and unconditional. He never reminded her of any of the stories she told him. Only *she* would start a conversation along those lines. Clayton understood her need to air and purge. He listened, and would make an understanding comment here and there, but never made judgments about her, or the men she'd been with. Always, he would lean forward and gently kiss her lips at the end of one of those long sad stories; his own way of closing and sealing that segment of her life. He always said she was as sweet as pie, and pie was his favorite thing to have. He could have pie at any time of day, at any temperature. He could have it with coffee, tea, or ice cream. It didn't matter. It was just that good, and that was his Cora. As much as Cora was aware of all these positive aspects in her relationship with Clayton Sax, she also knew that Mike had had the best of her heart, and feared that he would probably have it forever; not something she wanted at all. In her conscious mind, she had nothing but hatred for Mike and she knew that Clayton deserved more than she was giving him, just for loving her without reservation.

That night Clayton didn't stick around when he took Cora home. It was now quite late in the evening, and it was beginning to drizzle again. He wanted to get home and get a full night's sleep. His marriage proposal had been rejected one more time. In a strange way, he knew it was not really a rejection of who he was, but it hurt him all the same. He saw Cora in, kissed her goodnight and left wondering why she wasn't ready to marry him after all this time. His parents had been upstanding people in their community, and had passed on their sound values about doing the right thing by others, working hard, doing one's best under all circumstances. They had been hard workers themselves, and saw to it that their children made it to college to earn degrees without having to work during the day and study all night the way they had had to do. In fact, Clayton's dad had always joked with his mom that in marrying her he had married up, because when as a young man he had had a single pair of shoes, she had several pairs, one of which was gold with a 'diamond' bow at the front. Their children would do better. And they all had. Emily became the principal of a prestigious magnet school for the Arts; the twins, Joshua and Jonathan, became lawyers and owned a well established law firm together. Sax and Sax, Barristers at Law, had earned a pretty nice reputation for themselves. They were clean and fair-minded lawyers, determined to serve their clients' best interests without resorting to shady business, and they succeeded in doing just that. They ran a profitable and well-respected firm. In many cases profitable and well-respected were mutually exclusive terms. Not here. Clayton, the youngest, was the most studious as a child, graduated college a year early with a degree in aviation technology, was eagerly snatched up by IBM, and rose through their executive ranks with lightning speed. Still, Clayton felt that he was a notch below—despite his upbringing and achievements. He was one of only two unmarried executives at his branch. Before he met Cora, he had dated several women, but they didn't quite make the cut as wife material. They sought him out and wooed him, but he knew with that certainty of male radar, second only to woman's intuition, that they had been more interested in his assets and potential than in him. That's something his mom had frequently talked to him about as he became more and more successful. "Choose a woman for her goodness, Son." She had said to him time and time again. "Marry someone who would stick by you; someone who wants you for you." Cora was just like that, and Clayton wanted her. While she was always interested in his work and excited about his accomplishments, it was never about the money that came with it. She was just happy when he was happy. That made him feel worthy and loved. He didn't understand the hesitancy with the marriage thing, but maybe he could wait. She would be ready at some point to seal this thing up so he could breathe easy—not for his own relief, but for hers. Marrying her would guarantee that men could not hurt her like they had in the past. She would be his to love, honor, cherish, and protect 'til death did they part. She was someone he would stick by.

Back at home that evening, Cora took a long look at her face in the mirror. She was still unwrinkled, except for a few tiny lines at the corners of her eyes. *"Crow's feet!"* She heard herself say out loud. She remembered with a faint smile the very first time someone had called her ma'am. It happened one day in the supermarket. Some teenage boy had called her that. She hadn't exactly taken offense, but she thought about it for a long time, finally accepting the fact that maybe her age was beginning to show. She'd always thought that she looked ten years younger than she was, but maybe that was her own delusion. Maybe everyone else placed her within a year or two of her actual age just by looking at her.

She thought about Clayton and knew she had found the best man she could. Apart from being a strapping and striking six-foot-two, handsome, successful, really intelligent, well-spoken man (that last feature being something that held great attraction for her in choosing men), Clayton was someone she could stick by. If he asked her to marry him again she would say yes and seal this thing up so she could breathe easy. "Choose a man who loves you." Her Dad had told her as a girl. "Marry someone who would always be true to you." Clayton loved her like that. Cora considered herself a pretty lucky woman. She had been adopted as a baby and the couple that raised her had given her the finest possible upbringing and education, and every opportunity to create a great life for herself. Her heart was full of gratitude. Now she had found Clayton, and he was a gem—a keeper. She slid into her pajamas without showering again and climbed into bed, pulling the luxurious one thousand thread count, peach-colored, Pima cotton sheets up around her shoulders. These linens felt soft and wonderful against her skin, she thought, as she felt Clayton's love wash all over her. She wanted to drift into a peaceful sleep without losing any of that warmth and peace. Julia crossed her mind for a second. She knew her daughter must be somewhere in the house. She had heard her car pull into the driveway just as Clayton was about to leave. Cora knew that Julia had not come in to say hello because she thought that Clayton was around, and wanted to give her mother and him some space and privacy.

Julia had probably pulled in right before Clayton left, had seen his car out front, and had gone straight to her room. She might even have gone to the basement which had its own entrance, and was watching TV in the family room, Cora reasoned. There was no need to get up and check. They would catch up with each other over breakfast tomorrow. The two made a point of having breakfast together every morning. It was the way they experienced and provided feelings of warmth and security for each other. It was the way they tried to tune into each other every day. They connected in the morning. The rest of the day took them down separate paths, but mornings were their time. That routine seemed to work for both of them.

Chapter 2

On that drizzly June evening, while Cora drifted into a dreamless sleep after having been kissed goodnight by Clayton, Julia was raped in the basement of her mother's house.

In between the fiendish thrusting of the rapist's penis into her virgin flesh, he told her that he loved her more than anything in the world, had wanted her since the first time he saw her, didn't wish to be with anyone else, had imagined what taking her physically would feel like hundreds of times, and could not wait any longer—plain and simple.

When that act of violation was finally over, Julia dragged herself upstairs to her room, showered, and slid under her sheets without waking her mother.

That night, Julia slept fitfully and dreamt that she was raped.

Chapter 3

In the mail, two days later, Julia received an anonymously written poem in handwriting she didn't recognize. It read:

But then Love is
That abandonment of self—
As in those moments when
Two souls merge
And there's no knowledge
Of who you are,
Nor care
To find out;
Those moments when you know
Nothing
And everything
All at once;
When the whole world is at once in you
And far away from you;
When the mind is still,

But omniscient.
When your eyes reflect her being
And hers yours...
Either way, and both.
When there's neither smell nor taste.
When hearing is done by the soul,
And touching is through spirit;
When seeing the entire universe happens
As you look into the one pair of eyes
Locked with yours
And realize
Somewhere in the subconscious
That body's senses are too many for the moment,
Since you have need of only
Soul's hearing
Spirit's touching
And the eyes that capture
The entire universe...
Though one (eye)
Would do as well.
That
Love
Is.

Julia's head swam. She intuitively knew who had sent it although there was no name attached to the poem, and she didn't recognize the handwriting. Oh, the nerve of him! What was all this about souls merging? That was *not* what had happened three nights ago. Their souls had not merged, and she most certainly had not been touched by his spirit.

Instead, his body had forcefully entered hers against her wishes, and now she ached between her legs from the incessant thrusting, and ached in her heart from the violation. She was too ashamed to tell her mother, so she decided she would just have to deal with it alone. In time, the hurt would go away. Maybe she could confront her rapist, but she really couldn't risk being alone with him now.

Julia put the poem in the back left corner of her lingerie drawer, walked into the bathroom, turned on the shower and stood under the spray; her tears mixing with the warm, soothing water. She did not know how long she had been standing there, but now there was banging on the bathroom door, and Cora's voice was asking if everything was okay. In a deliberate effort at misleading her mother, Julia called out, "Oh, Yessss," and turned the showerhead to the *Massage* feature, which in that particular bathroom, made a whole lot of noise. The water hit the floor real hard, and a whistling sound started right up. With the massage feature on, the entire neighborhood probably knew that a shower was in use somewhere near them. Cora thought nothing of Julia's response. She had not expected a different response, really. She walked back to her bedroom across the hall and closed the door.

Julia's tears came faster now. Couldn't her mother tell that everything was *not* okay? Why hadn't she checked on her that evening three days ago? This was twice in three days that her mother had not been tuned in to her need for help. The sound of her mother's voice might have stopped her aggressor in the middle of this violent act. If only she had tried to find her, or had called out her name. Julia had tried to mentally send a message to her mother as her attacker pushed her down on the sofa and yanked off her blouse. She had thought that help would come and she would be delivered from this evil, but that didn't happen. Where was that mother's sixth sense that kicks in when her children are in danger? Were she and her mom so disconnected? Julia knew that her mother and herself did not share the same kind of closeness or friendship that some of her girlfriends shared with their mothers, despite their conscious effort to tune in to each other. They loved each other, and that love was unconditional, but they stuck to their roles. Their positions in the relationship were not interchangeable or negotiable. Cora was the mother, Julia was the daughter, and that was that; so at a time like this, Julia expected to be mothered, protected, and saved. How could Cora not have known that her daughter was in trouble was a question that would haunt her the rest of her life, Julia just knew, as she felt her heart break right down the middle and fall in two pieces to the bottom of her stomach.

Cora's not having any notion of her daughter's needs would not quite cause them to become estranged, but it would taint the trust; as far as Julia was concerned, anyway. It would also introduce to Julia the idea that there was no one in the world she could completely rely on. Theirs had always been a family of just the two of them, so relying on each other was supposed to be a given. Cora had explained to Julia quite early in the game that she had split with the man who had fathered her while she was still pregnant, and that he had moved away before she was born. Cora had made no promise to arrange a meeting for them, nor had she told her daughter who her father was. In fact, she stated that they were completely out of touch, had not seen each other or spoken since he left, and Julia had left it at that. The topic never came up again. The conversation between Cora and her daughter about the absent parent would cross Julia's mind occasionally, but not with any great degree of curiosity. Now as she thought about men, she wondered what kind of man left his child behind? How did her father walk so completely out of her mother's life, anyway? Was that what her mother wanted? Had he found someone else—a white woman, perhaps? Julia knew she was of mixed race, and figured that her father had most likely been caucasian. For a second, her mind turned to Clayton, and she wondered what kind of man doggedly pursued and remained emotionally attached to a woman who had refused to marry him several times? Cora had told Julia about each of Clayton's proposals, though she'd never asked her how she felt about them. Then about her most recent and horrible experience, Julia wondered: What kind of man raped a woman he professed to love? How many different kinds of men were there? At seventeen, could she figure out the truth about men? Was truth something different for everyone?

She felt her eyes begin to smart again as she turned the shower off, reached for a towel, stepped onto the rug, and began to dry herself off in front of the mirror. Julia buried her face in the towel to stifle her sobs, and hide her tears from herself.

"Oh, God!" she bawled into her towel, "What am I going to do?"

Chapter 4

Back on the boat, Gilbert hurried off the deck and back to his cabin to take a phone call that had just come in for him. Ken, or Cheffy, as he was fondly called by the crew, had come to him with a message that his son was on the phone. Which son it was, Ken didn't say. At some other time, Gilbert would have had a sarcastic remark to make to Ken about having been given too much information, or being as clear as mud, but not today. He hadn't heard from his sons in a while and he was eager to hear from either one of them. It had been six months since he had heard from Brock, his son by his first marriage, and not since then. He had quickly recognized his older son's voice on the phone. The call was brief. Brock told him that he had finished his pre-law degree at Columbia University in New York and would be taking the LSATs later that month. He told his father that his plans were to stay in New York. He really and truly liked it there. Straight out of high school, Brock had taken a clerical position in an accounting office in New York, and later on, found a job as an accountant with a prestigious law firm in that city. He worked as their accountant while pursuing a degree in the field. Being an ambitious young man and a quick learner, he soon started helping out in the pool of paralegals, in addition to doing the job that he was hired to do. After completing the accounting degree, Brock came to realize that he hated being an accountant, loved the legal aspect of things, and decided to go back to school to study law. He was a little older now, but he thought age and experience gave him an edge, and so he pursued his legal studies with fervor and enthusiasm, and did extremely well. Brock thoroughly enjoyed New York. He thought that city had everything to love.

"When you live in New York there's nothing to miss." Brock told his father, whose only response to his son's enthusiasm for the place was the brilliant quote that "fools rush madly where angels fear to tread." Brock had chuckled and given his father's comment no further thought. The pace in New York was fast; folks there had grand ideas about life. Brock thought the opportunities for spreading his wings were limitless. The little restaurants in SoHo were some of his favorite places to hang out after a busy day, or to "melt down the stress" as he preferred to say. He enjoyed the cultural diversity of the people who lived in the city, the plethora of ethnic foods, the sidewalk vendors, the deft artists who sketched the face of anyone who was willing to sit for ten minutes, the lone steel pan musician whose music on one corner blended with the music of the young, practicing saxophonist on the other end. He didn't understand how one could isolate oneself on a ship in the middle of the ocean, and deal with the same few personalities every day the way his father did. When he was in a more culturally elevated frame of mind, Broadway was Brock's place of choice, or Carnegie Hall. If a favorite of his, like Elton John, were playing Radio City Music Hall, then that would be the place for him. It would be Central Park's *Tavern on the Green* for dinner tonight, and a hot parmesan/herb pretzel from *Marty's* next to the newspaper stand on 29th street and 7th Avenue tomorrow night. He liked everything about the city equally well. For his dates with gorgeous women, it was usually the

Russian Tea Room. Oh! That perpetual feeling of change, of newness, of Joie de Vivre that New York unselfishly offered! Brock also enjoyed being in his late forties and still single. In fact, he considered himself a kind of modern day Alfred Kinsey in that he was able to think of sex as separate from love. The women he interacted with did not find his ideas on that matter very attractive, but they took their chances with him. Each dame thought that she might just be the one to make his commitment hormones kick in. Every man had those. It was just that the little buggers were in a deep sleep most of the time, waiting to be awakened by the right woman. There were so few men of that age who were still available, or who were not carrying around baggage from a previous wife and children, and the thought of his one day being a lawyer with his own practice made him all the more attractive to them. To think that one could find a catch like that in the heart of New York City!

Gilbert had called his son Charlie on the same day he heard from Brock and told him that he wished they could spend some time together. He had divorced Charlie's mom when the boy was six and had been in touch with him off and on over the years, but now Gilbert wanted something more. Charlie was now at an age where he could use the guidance of his father; or so Gilbert thought. There was money that Charlie could have from his rich dad; there was advice that he could certainly use in regard to school and considerations for a future career. However, it was friendship with Charlie that Gilbert really craved. His second son could be a great buddy. Maybe he, too, had a love of the ocean. He would show him the ropes, literally. They could hang out together. Gilbert hardly knew Brock at all, not having participated in his life except for sending birthday cards when the child was young, and the occasional conversation when he was older. Charlie, much younger, had met his older brother only once. The two had met on the yacht for a week one summer at Gilbert's request, and had displayed a mutual lack of interest in bonding. The energy it would take to get all three of them closely knit, Gilbert didn't think he had. The age difference between the boys probably created too large a gap to be closed anyway. He would try to draw in Charlie and leave Brock to his big-city lifestyle in Gotham. Lately, Gilbert had been feeling the need to be close to at least one of his sons. Over the years on board the ship, he had forged a close relationship with Ken, the chef on board his vessel, but it was a relationship of a completely different nature. Ken and he had become lovers two months after Ken started working on board *The Big Payoff*, and had been lovers ever since. The two men had felt an immediate though indefinable kinship, although not much had been exchanged between them by way of conversation. Then late one night, somewhere between Calais and Dover, after guzzling several bottles of chardonnay, each man told his secret to the other. They had both tried their hearts at loving women, but had failed miserably. Now they wanted men. A short distance away, Thelma, made ill by the undulating motion of the ship on the ocean, vomited. The two men watched her throw up and carefully move her feet away from the puddle of puke she had made on the floor, too spent to do anything more than that. Ken commented casually to Gilbert that people spilled their guts in all kinds of ways and for all kinds of reasons. The two exchanged a wink and a smile, and retired to their separate quarters. There was something about the senior gentleman that Ken deeply admired. Later that same night Gilbert made his way to the younger man's cabin. Ken was surprised to see Gilbert when he answered the knock on his door, but didn't ask him why he had come. Within seconds, the two had locked their lips together and frantically sought each other's tongue. Gilbert, feeling Ken's erection on his left thigh, undid his own zipper and eased a large, firm phallus out of his pants. Ken immediately dropped to his knees and took the older man into his mouth. When Gilbert exploded in ecstasy several minutes later and tried to return the favor, Ken refused. He was happy enough just knowing that he could make this man come. It was the beginning of a torrid love affair between the two, and they both thought that nothing could put an end to their love.

Over the next few months Ken learned much about the life of his lover. The younger man had stories of his own, but it was Gilbert's life that was full of wonder and adventure. Ken was always awestruck by his lover's stories, and thought his friend could have been a poster child for the concept *"Been there; done that."*

Chapter 5

As a young man not long out of high school, Gilbert had married Deborah Brinkley. He put off going to college to work at a real estate office, and toyed with the idea of becoming a broker and a millionaire at an early age. He figured that he would eventually become a mogul, widely traveled, well read, and filthy rich. That was his dream. Deborah, his high school sweetheart, had become pregnant with her son, Brock, after Gilbert and she returned from a wedding reception one night. In the wedding party, he had been an usher, she a bridesmaid, and they had spent the evening at the reception dancing closely and working up some heat between them. When Gilbert learned about the pregnancy, he did the right thing by Deborah. It hadn't been *his* idea. Deborah's father, loaded gun in hand, had threatened to kill both Gilbert and his daughter if there wasn't a speedy wedding to "fix this thing" as he put it. He gave the youngsters twenty-one days and a few thousand dollars, and they married hastily in Las Vegas; literally had a shotgun wedding.

The two remained married for one year, and divorced. Deborah refused child support and reverted to her maiden name, which she subsequently gave to Brock. Her parents moved her back into their spacious house and unflinchingly provided financial support for her and their beloved grandchild. The senior Brinkleys had no trouble explaining to their friends that their daughter was now divorced and living at home again. She was their only child, and there was no better place for her to be at this time in her life. Their daughter's living at home as a single, unwed rather than divorced mother would have been a totally different story, and not such a good one to tell, in their opinion. Their affluent friends would certainly think they had done something wrong in her upbringing, hence the unfortunate outcome of an illegitimate child. Taking her in after her divorce, was what good parents would do, especially for an only child. The Brinkleys remained noble and blameless in the eyes of their friends and acquaintances.

Gilbert did not object to the Brinkleys' arrangements for their daughter and grandson at all. In fact, he considered it a blessing.

He was a young man who needed to fend for himself in the world. He had a great interest in real estate, and aimed to be financially independent at an early age. He would keep in touch with his son as much as Deborah allowed. Maybe he and his son would be close when the child became older and didn't need his mother's authorization for phone calls and visits. They could somehow manage to have a father and son relationship. Well, that never happened. At first Brock and his father talked only when Gilbert called, and later, Brock would make the occasional call to say hello and give a bit of an update on his life or plans, never seeking his father's advice, opinions, or approval. He mentioned events in his life only as a matter of casual conversation; just kind of an FYI for Gilbert.

As years rolled by after the divorce and Deborah and his son moved further out of his life, Gilbert left them alone and pursued his dreams of becoming a real estate tycoon. He also became increasingly unsure of his sexuality but he continued to date casually, and eventually met another woman, Marlene, through a mutual friend. After dating her exclusively for about a year, he thought he loved her enough to marry her, and together they had Charlie. It was a relationship that would last eight years. When Charlie was born, two years into the marriage, Gilbert was sure it would strengthen his resolve to be heterosexual, and toss a ball around with his son in manly fashion. It didn't work; and so he found himself spending more and more time away from his family and becoming severely depressed. When he was at home, he interacted with Charlie to some degree, but had completely lost interest in Marlene. She felt his rejection, but didn't suspect that the problem was his. She thought she had probably grown unattractive or uninteresting to him. Maybe he had left his first marriage because he married too young and for the wrong reason. Her he loved, so she figured it had to be something she was doing wrong, or not doing well enough. Besides, Gilbert was her senior by 7 years. Men always adored a somewhat younger wife. She vowed to make her marriage work come Hell or High Water.

Hell came, and so did High Water, but the couple drifted farther apart. Gilbert stayed in the marriage six more years, watching Marlene in her one-sided effort at saving the marriage and knowing there was nothing she could do, but he didn't have the courage to tell her so. He knew that if he left her, she could find someone with whom to share her life; someone who would really love her. She was very beautiful, and relatively young. Marlene, though, never harbored these thoughts. Hell and High Water befriended Gilbert, too, and day after day he rehearsed with himself the speech that would call it quits for them.

Finally, he decided it was time to end the charade and leave the marriage. He had to be true to himself and fair to Marlene. She had been nothing but a wonderful wife to him, and a great mother to his son. Today was her birthday. He would give her the gift of truth, and freedom to have real love for the rest of her life.

Gilbert came home that night and told Marlene that he wanted, in fact, *had to have* a divorce. She didn't argue with him. She didn't even see the point in asking him why. She had been so deeply hurt by her husband's coldness and distance in the years that preceeded this event that she had become numb. In a low tone that sounded almost like she was talking to herself, Marlene heard herself say, "If that's what you want, it's okay with me."

In the years that followed his departure from the marriage, Gilbert tried to stay in touch with his son but their relationship was never quite what it should be. He sent child support to Marlene and would call the house to speak with Charlie on holidays, or on his birthday when the boy was young. Marlene never had Charlie make any calls to Gilbert. When Charlie was older, he kept up polite dealings with his father on a schedule that was comfortable for himself. He would respond to Gilbert's letters in his own time, stating that all was well with him and Mom, and that he hoped things were great for his dad. He had a phone number for his father, but didn't use it much. When Marlene gave Charlie his own telephone line, Gilbert was not one of the people to whom Charlie gave the number. Calls to Charlie from his father continued to come through on Marlene's land line. Marlene would call Charlie to the phone or leave him a message that his father had called. Apart from these phone calls, about two brief letters a year were all that Charlie and Gilbert shared.

When he left this second marriage, Gilbert had a sense of having lost a lot. This was his second marriage down the tubes and second alienated son. However, he felt that Paradise could be regained if he could live outside the lie of the previous years, and be himself. After all, the truth was supposed to set one free. He was sure there would be an opportunity at some point in the future to explain things to his child. His need to live as a homosexual male did not diminish his fatherly love for his son in any way. Charlie needed to know that. Maybe, later.

Chapter 6

Charlie, as a boy, seemed even-tempered and well adjusted. His mother did her best to make up for the absence of his dad, and there was enough money coming in from Gilbert to keep them in a very comfortable lifestyle. In high school the young man was the captain of his hockey team and his striking good looks and athletic physique made him quite the dream of all the girls—cheerleaders and ugly ducklings alike. He was charming, too. He smiled easily and seemed sure of himself in a nonchalant sort of way. In his senior year, Julia Jenkins had caught his eye and no one had been able to distract him since then, although he was generally friendly toward the other females who swarmed like bees around him. Even when he had been asked by one of the school's most popular blondes what he saw in Julia who wasn't even of his own race, he had good naturedly responded that he simply loved everything about her and *then* some. The girl had looked him over, tossed her bouncy, blonde mane and walked away with a haughty attitude, which only made Charlie smile. At home that night he composed a poem which he glued to the young lady's locker the following day:

I thought I would
Create a poem for you,
Something that befits both
Your beauty and your sense of self;
For just as we were meshed in conversation,
I thought I saw something of the other in you...
A somewhat sisterness...
An almost twinship in the style and poise
Of her whom I love
And you.
But then you blew it with the ugly attitude.

As Charlie walked away he wondered why he had even gone through the trouble to do this. Did he wish to appease or torment this girl? Would the poem compound her hurt or give her hope? He told himself that it was being done just for fun, but somewhere deep inside himself he felt that he had meant it as a slap in the face. He remembered that he had gone back and inserted the words *somewhat* and *almost* after he had finished writing the poem. He wanted to let her know that she hadn't managed to get his attention the way Julia had, though she might have been close. This was the slightly sinister side of himself that only *he* knew about. He was always overtly and verbally pleasant, but sometimes he felt a semi-dormant current of desire to hurt others running through him. He spoke only to himself about that because it made him a little uneasy. Once he had inflicted the pain, however, he felt a thrill, and then a sense of calmness again—at least for a while. He had heard people talk of *Dr. Jekyll and Mr. Hyde;* he had watched the movies *Three Faces of Eve*, and *The Color of Night*. He felt that there were two different sides to his personality, but he didn't think that it was cause for major concern, and decided not to mention it to other people in his life. He certainly would not discuss the matter with his mother. She would make way too much of it. She would probably want him to go to therapy. She was still in therapy herself; started going after her divorce. Charlie had also heard of people who were bipolar, but he thought that the duality he occasionally felt was so mild, that it couldn't possibly be the case with him. Besides, his "episodes of evil" didn't last long. It was not that big a deal, really. Maybe it was the confusion of his adolescent years. Anyway, it wasn't posing a major problem at home or in school at this point.

By all appearances Charlie was the ultimate catch: Smart, well off, good-natured, tall, and handsome. What else could anyone hope to be or want? None of his friends had anything on him. In fact, they joked with him about needing tips on how to win the hearts of women with no effort at all. What more could a guy ask for? Charlie was very happy with his life. His mother had told him the story of her life with his father, Gilbert; how she had struggled to save the relationship, and how he finally broke the news of his homosexuality to her, but Charlie didn't think it affected his own life in any way. That was his parents' issue. It really had nothing to do with him at all; not in a real sense. However, he did wonder what on earth had gotten into him the night that he raped Julia.

He felt sick to his stomach as anguish and regret filled his soul. He sat down on the floor abruptly, near the end locker in the school's long corridor, put his head between his hands, and tried to recall the sequence of events on the night he raped his girlfriend in the basement of her mother's house, right there on the sofa. His eyes felt hot as they filled up with tears, and he permitted a single drop to roll down his cheek. He dried it up with the back of his hand. He decided to cut the rest of his classes today. He had to go home right away. He needed to call his father.

Chapter 7

These nights, Julia's sleep was short and fitful at best. She would fall asleep easily because she was mentally exhausted and emotionally spent, but would wake up after about three hours and spend the rest of the night swamped with feelings of hurt, regret, fear, shame, and insurmountable anxiety. She felt that some action needed to be taken but she had no idea what to do, where to go, or whom to tell about what was troubling her. While she thought that she should probably confront Charlie, she knew she couldn't bring herself to look at him at all. Intellectually she knew she had no guilt to bear, but there was that pang of shame, of hurt, of feeling stupid, unworthy, permanently ruined somehow. Did her anguish show on her face? Did she smile a joyless smile? Was there pain in her eyes? Could her friends tell that she was hiding something? Did strangers know that she was dirty? She must leave this town now. The anonymity she could hide behind in a new place might be the solution to her problems; at least a distraction from what seemed to be this new disgusting aspect of her self.

Tonight was no different. Julia had gone to bed early and awakened in a cold sweat. She lay there and felt the panic in her head; felt her heart pounding against her ribcage. In a sudden move she was out of bed and headed for her mother's bedroom. Cora's door was always unlocked. Even when Clayton was around the door remained unlocked, although closed. Cora would make sure that Julia knew there was company, but never locked her daughter out. Julia knew how things worked. If she came home after her mother and Clayton were in the house, his coat would be carelessly thrown on the armchair in the living room, or his keys would be on the dining table. The living room and dining room adjoined each other and veered off into the kitchen in an open floor plan. If Julia was home when Cora and Clayton arrived, they would chat with her for a minute before going to sit in the den, and after Julia had said goodnight to them and gone to her room, they would retire to Cora's bedroom. Julia knew that Cora was alone in her bed tonight, and felt that she had to talk to her then and now. She quietly opened the bedroom door and slid into bed next to her mother. Cora inched over without waking up. For a moment, Julia lay in her mother's bed silently; her face against her mother's back. Maybe she would wait 'til morning to talk to her. However, one minute later, she was shaking her mother awake. Cora sat up, rubbed her eyes and turned slowly toward her daughter who was now also sitting up.

"I'm leaving for Paris in a week, Mom," Julia said without preamble. "I think it will take me that long to make the arrangements for a place to stay over there." Julia now shifted her position to look directly at her mother.

"I'll stay there a couple of months while I think a few things through. You'll be okay, won't you?"

Cora stared at her daughter whose face she could barely see in the semi-darkness of the room. Neither one of them spoke for several seconds.

"Talk to me, Julia. Start over." Cora was finally able to say.

"I can't get into it now," Julia said. "I'll explain it all later. I just must get away real soon. I *must* go far away from here. I promise I'll explain it all later. You trust me, don't you?"

"Sure I do." Cora assured her daughter. "Sure I do."

The two now lay down on their backs and Julia put her head in the space between her mother's chin and shoulder and drifted off to sleep. Cora listened to her daughter's even breathing and wondered what on earth had just happened. She knew she had not been dreaming. Maybe this would clear itself up in the morning. After lying with her eyes closed for what could have been fifteen minutes, Cora realized that she could not go back to sleep, but she didn't move for fear of waking Julia. She thought about her daughter, herself, her daughter's future, her own future. She let her mind revisit conversations and experiences with the men who had been in her life. Now she thought more than ever about Julia's father, and wondered how different life would have been for the three of them if they had formed a nuclear family. She thought about him, and wondered where he was. He was, after all, the father of her child, but she had not kept track of his whereabouts the way she had kept track of Mike's. She knew where Mike was and what he was up to at all times, just about.

Chapter 8

Ken Rudolph had never married; in fact, he had not been with a woman since leaving Cora Jenkins. They had dated for over a year, almost a year and a half, and then it was suddenly over. Cora and he had met in France. In those days Ken had noticed that when he was with Cora he didn't really feel that chemistry or sexual arousal that he thought he should, although he knew that his initial attraction to her was a physical one. He remembered the day she walked by him at the Louvre in Paris, and he had felt uneasy in his pants. It hadn't happened again when he was around her, but he really did like her very much. They were together almost everyday, though they kept their own apartments. They dated, cuddled, kissed, and fondled, but nothing more. One evening when they were together at her place, he mentioned something about her having a whole lot going for her, and said he was sure she could find a wonderful man. Cora was surprised by the statement, but did not press for an explanation at the time. They went into the kitchen, cooked together, a simple dinner of fingerling potatoes and salmon. He found the makings of a salad in the refrigerator, and put them together. They ate dinner and made light, pleasant conversation. After dinner, the two moved to the living room and played a few board games while they shared a pint of Chunkey Monkey, Ken's favorite flavor of Ben and Jerry's ice cream. Cora had put a little of it into an ice-cream dish for herself; he spooned his share directly out of the container into his mouth.

The time went by very quickly and before they knew it, several hours had flown by. Suddenly noticing that it was midnight, Ken told Cora that he would spend the night. She was somewhat miffed by the decision, remembering his earlier comment which seemed to be his way of saying he didn't want a committed relationship with her, but she decided not to comment on either his earlier remark or this last, out-of-a-clear-blue-sky decision. Ken pulled the navy Ralph Lauren polo shirt over his head to remove it, and Cora admired his handsome physique as he slowly ascended the stairs. She heard him go into her bedroom and then into her bathroom. She noted how comfortable she felt having him in her space.

I guess I should go to bed myself. It's great that he's staying over. Something about him feels right in my space, Cora thought in a whisper to herself.

She put away the games, turned off the lights, and began climbing the stairs to her bedroom. Half way up she decided to make sure that she knew where her keys were, and came down again. She didn't want to have to scurry around looking for them in the morning when she was ready to leave the house. That was her pattern. The keys were, as she thought she'd remembered, on the kitchen counter. She ascended the stairs one more time.

Upstairs in her bedroom, Cora peeled off her clothes and walked into the bathroom to drop them in the hamper. Catching a glimpse of Ken's silhouette through the frosted glass of the shower door, something stirred in her, and she made the spontaneous decision to join him. He turned and smiled at her as she entered naked into the shower, continuing to lather himself with sensuous movements of his hands over his chiseled frame.

Seeing his smile, she immediately began to caress his torso, and very soon was guiding his turgid penis into her body. She caught her breath as he entered her, and hoisted herself up, wrapping her legs around his hips. For several minutes, he thrust his rock-hard penis into the moistness between her legs, his every move made even more exhilarating to Cora by the warm spray of the shower. He fucked her slowly at first, then faster and more passionately. Cora felt her vulva become engorged and thought the sweet ache in her vagina would make her heart stop. She was moaning loudly now. Encouraged by her moans and the heat of her mouth on his neck, he fucked her hard; his hands pressed into the cheeks of her buttocks. He loved their firmness, and let himself feel every ridge and fold of her vagina as he moved in and out of her. He felt her nails on his back now, and he fucked her harder still. Moments later, his own heavy breathing mingled with her sighs, and his body shook as he spilled his cum deep inside her. Slowly he pulled his penis out of her, slid her legs down from around his hips, quickly rinsed himself, and stepped out of the shower without looking at her. Cora lingered in the shower a few minutes longer letting the warm spray of water hit her clitoris until she brought herself to a climax. By the time she came out of the bathroom, Ken was asleep in her bed.

It was in that single act of brazenness on her part and surrender on his, that Cora conceived her daughter, Julia.

Chapter 9

At first Gilbert was happy to hear Charlie's voice at the other end of the line, but he soon realized that his son was furious. The slow, calculated way in which Charlie spoke, let Gilbert know that something was radically wrong.

"This is your son." He began. "I thought I'd let you know that three nights ago I raped my girlfriend, Julia Jenkins. I wanted to be sure that I wasn't gay, Dad. She was making me wait, and while I waited I wondered about myself. I knew that I wanted her, but there were male friends of mine I thought I wanted that way, too. I needed to find out who or what I was. I know about you. Mom thought I should know that there was nothing she could have done to save the marriage so she told me the whole story. You knew you were gay, or bisexual or something, before you married her, but did anyway. Was that selfish, Dad? Or was that selfish? Did you think Mom could be the cure? Julia was a beautiful girl before this mishap, and I do think it was a mishap. I felt pure horror as I watched her beautiful honey-colored skin turn pale with fear and terror. She stuffed her own hair into her mouth to quiet her sobs. I spoke gently to her all through it, trying to feel the joy I had imagined before actually taking her, but there was none. I told her that I loved her all through that horrendous act, but I could see only fear and confusion in her eyes. You ruined it for me, Dad. You gave life to a freak like yourself. All these years, I tried to keep things between us civil—only for my mother's sake. I knew there was a reason I didn't like you, but I couldn't put my finger on it. Now that I've ruined my life and Julia's, I finally know for sure that I absolutely hate you. Good-bye Gilbert Jacob. Good-bye. I wish I could say that it was nice knowing you, but I regret that I was even born. Goodbye."

The phone went dead before Gilbert could process what he had just heard, or respond to his son. There had been no pause during Charlie's tirade for questions or comments from the older man.

For several seconds longer, Gilbert held the receiver to his ear—not hearing anything; not speaking into it; unable to think clearly, or stop the sting of the tears that were quickly filling his eyes.

As Charlie hung up the phone and bolted up to his room taking two stairs at a time, he could hear a poem starting in his head:

Oh, hasten Death, and rid me of
The burdens that I bear...
Just take me to a better place...

"I don't have the nerve to finish this one." He heard his own voice quietly say. His mind suddenly moved to the 38 Caliber Stub Nose he kept hidden in the bottom drawer of his dresser. It had been a gift from Jake, a senior at his school whose father was an avid gun collector and boasted a large assortment of those weapons. Charlie was thinking that he hadn't polished the thing in a while. He would do that right now. The small bottle of silver polish was on the other side of the same drawer, wrapped in tinfoil and pushed way to the back.

"One should keep one's gun loaded, shiny, and ready," he mused, as he reached into the drawer and felt the cool metal at the tips of his fingers.

Chapter 10

Julia sat down to breakfast with Cora. It was a beautiful morning and the midnight mystery she had created in her mother's mind seemed far away. She debated with herself whether or not to tell her mother what she'd been hiding. She could relieve her pain by telling her mom everything: about the rape, the poem, Charlie, her mother's own blindness to her pain, her decision to go to Paris for a while, but she would first gauge her mother's frame of mind. She didn't want to upset her, although more than anything, she needed her comfort. Cora, on the other hand, breathed short breaths and tried not to look anxious, but she couldn't wait to hear what last night was all about. She resolved to keep her calm and wait until her daughter wanted to talk about it.

"It's nice to know we could both just live on eggs and toast if we had to." Cora began, taking a hearty bite of her toast and trying not to be the one to bring up the bizarre midnight episode they had both just been a part of. She winked playfully at her daughter.

"I guess." Julia replied, shifting her gaze from her mother's eyes.

This conversation, Julia knew now, would have to wait for another time; maybe it would never happen. She would have to seek solace from herself for now. It confirmed for Julia her initial suspicion that maybe there was no one in the world she could really count on. That initial suspicion now seemed to be a hurtful reality. She didn't want that truth settling in her soul; she wanted to think that she was somehow mistaken, had jumped too quickly to that conclusion, but somewhere in her heart she knew that she was right. A tight knot of pain rose up in the center of her throat and spread itself in a thin line on both sides of her neck like a strand of pearls waiting to be fastened. In her mind's eye she saw herself standing alone in the middle of the planet, without comfort or understanding from any one; without the curiosity of a friend, without even a connection to her mother. Wasn't a mother's love the most love that anyone was ever guaranteed? What had happened between them that had cheated her out of that? Julia almost choked on the next piece of toast that she bit into, and decided that breakfast was over. She placed her set of dishes in the sink, and without a word to Cora, shot up the stairs to her room.

Blinded by the tears that were now streaming down her face in an unbroken line, she threw herself in the middle of her bed and bawled uncontrollably into the mattress.

Chapter 11

Alone in his room, Charlie smiled at himself in the full-length mahogany mirror that was tilted against the bedroom wall nearest the door, put the freshly polished, loaded revolver into his open mouth, and pulled the trigger.

His mother, Marlene Jacob, nestled comfortably on the gold, chenille-upholstered sofa in the family room, did not hear the gun shot that went into the base of her son's brain, nor did she hear the thud of his body as he fell backwards on the floor.

She continued leisurely leafing through the latest issue of *Marie Claire*.

Chapter 12

Back at school later that day, news of Charlie's death spread like wildfire, but details were unknown. Marlene had decided to knock on her son's bedroom door, not having seen him for several hours, and knowing that he hadn't left the house. He always said that he was leaving and would soon be back when his mother was around. When there was no response from him after several seconds, she turned the door knob, quietly calling his name as she slowly pushed the door open.

"Oh, my *God*!" Marlene gasped at the sight of Charlie's body on the floor. "Oh, my God. Charlie! Charlie."

She shook her son and then put her fingers to his neck to feel for a pulse. There was none. She put her hand on his stomach to see if he was breathing. There was no breath. Charlie's body was lifeless.

How long Marlene remained in a faint, she didn't know. When she regained consciousness, she walked out of the room, stood at the top of the stairs for a moment to steady herself, and then began to slowly descend the stairs to the kitchen, holding on to the railing as she walked in order to keep her balance. Once in the kitchen, she lifted the cordless receiver out of its cradle, leaned her back up against the refrigerator, dialed 911 to say that she thought her son was dead and would like someone to come, called her neighbor to say that she'd found Charlie dead in his room and didn't know what had happened, and called her son's school to say that he had died and wouldn't be in. She did not, however, think of calling Charlie's father, Gilbert, with the news.

Because Marlene did not make that call to her son's father, it would be several days before she found out that Gilbert had shot himself to death on his boat shortly after receiving a phone call from Charlie. Gilbert's suicide had been committed at about the same time as Charlie's. A note found in Gilbert's shirt pocket said thanks to Charlie for having called, and asked that Marlene, Charlie, and Brock be contacted after his body had been cremated and his ashes thrown into the sea. The note further asked that Ken take care of these matters, and anything else that needed to be handled, whether it was mentioned in the note, or not. Ken, after all, had been the person closest to Gilbert, and maybe there were matters that he, Gilbert, could not bring to mind now that would need to be taken care of after his death. Ken, his true friend and loyal paramour, would know exactly what to do.

Chapter 13

Ken Rudolph was at first stunned by his lover's suicide, then racked with pain, and then furious. For Gilbert to have actually taken his own life, for him to have done something so absolutely selfish, he must not have thought of him, his lover, at all. He had thought all along that they shared good times and bad. Was something so radically wrong that Gilbert couldn't talk to him about it? Nothing Gilbert could have divulged would have made Ken love him less! Was he gravely ill—something contagious maybe? Had he passed something on to his lover, and now could not bear the guilt of that? What on earth could make him take his own life—and without warning—like that? The answer had to lie in that phone call from Charlie, Ken suspected. Everything had been fine up to that point. What the hell had Gilbert and Charlie talked about that drove his friend to this?

What Thelma neglected to tell Ken when she broke the news of Gilbert's suicide, was that she had listened in on that earlier conversation between Charlie and his father. Thelma had known for a long time that the phone in her cabin had been set up to listen to, and tape all conversations that came to the ship, and replay them later. That room which was designated as Thelma's cabin when she joined the crew was originally Gilbert's office. He had had the bugging device installed when he first bought the ship, for the purpose of keeping tabs on his crew. As he grew to trust and love them, using the monitoring system had become unnecessary. Gilbert had not told Thelma about the device, and didn't think it was something he needed to ever worry about. Thelma, however, had discovered the system, quite by accident, and never let on that she had. She knew it would serve her purpose at some point in time. When? She didn't know then, but was guarded and calculating enough to keep that discovery to herself.

Ken downed a double scotch straight up, went to his cabin, lay across the bed, and hit the power button on the TV's remote control. The television screen lit up with a row of cars and something that looked, at a glance, like a red, white, and blue bunting. He hit the mute button. He lay there staring at the TV screen as pictures flashed off and on without registering anything. His mind was beginning to slow down, and he felt his eyelids becoming heavy. He decided that he would figure it all out after the shock was gone, or at least numbed, and allowed himself to fall asleep. There was anger in his mind, yes, but it was beginning to subside, and deep in his heart he felt more sadness than he thought he could possibly bear.

Thelma, on the other hand, silently thanked God for Gilbert's death. Forty-seven years earlier he had raped her during a house-warming party they had both attended for a mutual friend. Having had way too much Cristal, and ignoring Thelma's little speech about not wanting to sleep with someone she was not in a committed relationship with, Gilbert had forced himself on his friend. While their friends mingled and laughed in the great room, Gilbert dragged Thelma into an empty bedroom and raped her. She conceived a daughter whom she gave up for adoption the very day she was born.

Thelma had not coped well with that transaction. Once she saw her baby, she wanted to keep her, but the arrangements had already been made and she could not stand the thought of a long battle to get out of the contract. She suffered a nervous breakdown as a result of it, and was admitted to the psychiatric unit of the same hospital where she had delivered the baby three days earlier. Thelma was released from that ward after about three weeks, and spent her life in and out of short-term jobs, never quite having the capacity for the stressful situations and the corporate climbing that might have put her in a stable financial position. She had been, after all, one of the brighter minds at school, so the idea of success for her was not far-fetched, but she couldn't manage to get there.

Gilbert learned about the tragic results of that night's activity between Thelma and himself very many years later. He had run into old friends at an alumni fundraiser, and in mentioning people they had lost track of, Thelma's name had come up. Gillian, her best friend in high school and throughout college, had been in touch with her over all these years. She pulled Gilbert away from the others and walked him out to the balcony. Once there, Gillian told him that she knew all about the night he raped her friend and got her pregnant, but that she had been sworn to secrecy by Thelma. Since Thelma and she were best friends, she had kept that trust. Thelma had given birth to a daughter but had to give the baby up for adoption because she was unable to take care of her at the time. Her friend had suffered a nervous breakdown and had mended, sort of, but had never been quite herself after giving her daughter up for adoption, and being in that psychiatric unit. Thelma's case had not been so severe that she required residence at a mental hospital for an extended period of time, and she had not had to be re-hospitalized, but her life had been permanently altered. She was able to return to a "normal" life in her community, but these experiences had taken their toll. Gillian also told

Gilbert that the couple who, at the time, was about to become the adoptive parents of the baby had taken a liking to Thelma, and as a gesture of kindness and good will, allowed her to name her daughter. Thelma named her baby Cora, no middle name, just Cora. The couple's last name was Jenkins; that much she knew, but knew nothing else about them, or what eventually happened to the baby girl. Thelma had never mentioned the topic again, and Gillian had respectfully refrained from ever bringing it up. Gillian also let Gilbert know that as a result of that chain of unfortunate events, Thelma had not managed to establish any romantic relationships over the course of her life. She was depressed most of the time, socialized with no one but her best friend, and was in and out of different jobs, trying to keep herself afloat financially. Thelma never bought into the idea of going to therapy, either. She said that she was okay. Gillian just thought that, after all these years, Gilbert ought to know that his self-centered actions of a single night had drastically and negatively impacted her friend's life; in fact, had wrecked it completely.

Gilbert took in this news from Gillian without any obvious show of emotion or interest in the story, but there and then he vowed to find Thelma and do whatever he could to help her. He thought, too, of the daughter he just heard about, had never met; never knew existed. He wished for a moment that his life had taken a more traditional route: a heterosexual marriage, children by one woman, a stable job on land not far from home; but that was not for him, really, and he knew that. Out of a sense of obligation and some feeling of compassion for someone he had been quite chummy with in his youth, Gilbert decided that Thelma would have a job on his yacht, if she wanted that, so she could at least provide for herself with some degree of consistency and stability. He would help her regain her dignity and achieve some peace. Gilbert remembered that Thelma had always been considered a fine young woman by everyone who knew her. She was charming and witty, and had the potential to achieve anything she wanted in life. Some years earlier, Gilbert had planned on buying a yacht for his sixtieth birthday, but being Gilbert, a person who was always in need of immediate gratification, he had bought it years earlier; he had seen no reason to wait. He would find Thelma now, and make her a job offer with the following conditions: He would do what he could to get her on her feet; they would have no social interaction with each other on the boat, and would not tell anyone about their past, or the fact that somewhere out there was a daughter whose biological parents they both were, and Thelma could work on the *The Big Payoff* for as long as she wanted. He would let her know that he had no interest in tracking down this daughter of theirs. When he first learned of the child's existence, he had a spontaneous surge of emotion and felt that he wanted to know more about her, but within moments the fear of disrupting his own life and opening up new cans of worms for everyone far outweighed his curiosity. His parental instincts were both superficial and fleeting. He said a quick, silent prayer that his daughter's life was good and let the thought of her go, but Thelma, he felt he could help. He decided to stick around for another couple of days, and with a little legwork right there in their old hometown, he was able to locate Thelma. It took him exactly two days to find her. He had decided it was a bad idea to just ask Gillian to connect them, so he conducted the search himself; talking casually to folks he met and gathering as much information as he could. In small towns everyone knew everyone, and Gilbert knew well how that worked.

Thelma was surprised to see her child's father, but had grown so accustomed to presenting a poker face to everyone she met, that Gilbert saw no emotion in her at all, although she now thought he was a dead ringer for Nick Nolte, and still as attractive as he was all those years ago. Gilbert was not, however, put off by that show of coldness on Thelma's part. Gillian had told him that her friend was almost always depressed, so it made sense that Thelma did not jump for joy at seeing him. He got right to the point, and made her the offer he had come to make. As Thelma listened to Gilbert's terms and conditions for her life, she realized that this decision, just like the one he'd made on that fateful night all those years ago, was all about himself. Thelma also realized that there was no reason on earth she would want to share time and space with this man other than the fact that she was tired of going from job to job and having her checkbook constantly in the red, so she accepted his offer. She went back to her apartment where she lived on a month to month basis, packed her few possessions, unceremoniously turned her key in to the landlady, and left to begin work at this new job on Gilbert's ship. At that point, Thelma had no idea how long she would remain in that position. She would just play it all out by her gut.

Over the years of working in close physical proximity to Gilbert, literally under his nose, as he dictated his wishes and she copied them on a pad, Thelma often wondered if the name of his yacht had anything to do with the deal he had made with her. How long had he known about the baby? How long had it taken him to find her? Had he searched high and low for a long time? Was it a recent decision to care on his part? Or had he just heard the news right about the time when he approached her, and made a quick decision in his usual spontaneous manner? Was it just his way of eliminating his own guilt, and really not about compassion for her? She didn't know the answer to any of these questions, and certainly would not ask, but what a kick in the teeth it would be if the name of his ship was somehow tied to the offer he had made her! Maybe he *did* know about the baby and had planned this all out to somehow compensate for the damage he had caused in her life. Something kept telling her that this was the case; but then again, maybe not. She felt her confusion grow, but decided that the why of it didn't matter now. This job was an opportunity for her on several levels. She would have a steady income, she would see the world, or a lot of it (that had been one of her ambitions as a child), and she would be close to Gilbert *all the time.* She thought the job would provide a great opportunity to poison him during one of those elaborate dinner parties he had told her he held on board the ship. He had mentioned them as part of his sales pitch when he offered her the position. As he put it, she would get a chance to meet some new and interesting folks at his socials. It seemed to Thelma that Gilbert was giving her a perfect opportunity for revenge. Then and there, she vowed to kill him. What with all the people who came on board, no one would suspect her of having done anything. It would be the ultimate *WhoDoneIt,* if murder were suspected at all.

Years passed, but Thelma had not been successful at getting her plans to kill Gilbert accomplished. Her first attempt at murdering him was by mixing arsenic powder into his liver pâté. Thelma usually served Beluga caviar to the guests, and made liver pattè just for Gilbert because, as he explained it, he just preferred the taste of liver. The poisoned patte, however, had only made him sick to his stomach, and the vehement vomiting that followed had saved his life. Now that he had killed himself, (and she was sure he had done it with a certain degree of flair and arrogance), that was one less person she had to worry about removing from the world.

The crew members had each had an entirely different reaction to Gilbert's death. Ken had been clearly devastated by the news of his lover's demise. Thelma had been relieved. Clarence had reacted to the news with only a motion of the mouth that pushed his bottom lip out of alignment with his top lip, and a slight nod of the head. There was no legible expression in his eyes. It was as if someone had just told him it was raining.

Having broken the news to the two men on the ship, Thelma walked back to her cabin, stooped down, and removed a small gray box from under the bunk bed that was pushed up against the wall. She slowly opened the lid of the box and saw that the eight-groove 38-caliber revolver was still in it. She quickly closed the lid of the box and put it back in its place; she had no use for it now. But then again, "sometimes a girl just needs a gun," she mused. One never knows.

Chapter 14

At home, Julia packed for her trip to Paris. She had no intention of going back to school before leaving for Europe. Her mother would contact the school sometime later to inform them about her departure. She would write to Charlie from Paris, she thought, and tell him that she planned to live out of the United States for a while. It was not that she felt he deserved to have an explanation, but somehow she felt that a letter would elicit a response from him that might be of comfort to her. She was sure he would say how much it hurt him to have raped her. He would get her phone number from her mother, who of course would have no reason in the world not to give it to him, and hearing his voice again would soothe her. She would not be coming back to him, but she would know that he did not mean to disrespect or harm her. She was mildly disgusted by the thought of her seeking comfort from the very person who had hurt her, but that was what she felt she needed, and she wanted to do whatever it took to get rid of her pain. Charlie had once sent her a poem that began:

"I want to gather up the fragments of my soul...."

She wondered where the poem was. If she could find it she would take it with her to Paris. Maybe it would help her heal.

Busy with all the preparations to leave for Paris, neither Julia nor Cora had gotten news of Charlie's death. They were spending those last several hours together packing, talking about Paris, and just engaging in light hearted chitchat. Cora tried not to show that she was worried about Julia's going off to Europe alone. She reminded herself that she had friends in Paris who would look out for her daughter once she let them know that her child was there. Besides, Julia had always been a pretty mature and independent girl. Cora *did* think it strange that Julia had not mentioned anything about Charlie's response to her decision to spend so much time away, but she was never one to openly pry into her daughter's affairs. She preferred to watch from a distance, being anxious all the while about her daughter's experiences with men, but hiding it, and trying to figure out what she would do to save or protect her child, should it become necessary. She wondered how Charlie felt about Julia's leaving for an extended period, and thought there might have been a cooling of the relationship between them, but she never guessed there was serious trouble. Cora kept her thoughts on this matter to herself. Julia would bring up her personal life if she wanted to talk about it, and at that time, Cora's questions would be appropriate.

The big day came, and Julia left for France. On the way home from taking her daughter to the airport, Cora stopped off at Janvier Samorra just to browse. She spent a couple of hours there, looking at one item after another, slinging pocketbooks over her arm and turning around in front of the mirror to see how they looked on her. She looked at this, and looked at that, but nothing captured her interest. She was already missing Julia and this browsing was just an empty exercise to distract herself. She thought of stopping at FCUK's to do some more browsing, but decided that their ware was more Julia's style. Her teenage days were long past, so she skipped that store.

When she finally got home about 4 p.m. that afternoon, Cora put her purse down on the kitchen table and pressed the message button on the answering machine to see who had called. There was only one message. It was from one of Julia's classmates. It said:

"Julia, this is Pam. I know you won't be at school for a while due to Charlie's death. I'm really sorry. Call me if you feel like talking. Love ya!"

Cora felt her extremities turn cold, and she stood motionless for a while. She hit the repeat button and listened to the message again. She *did* hear what she thought she'd heard. She couldn't contact her daughter. Julia hadn't even gotten to Paris yet. It was at least a seven-hour flight there from Los Angeles. Besides, this was all the information she had. Pam had not left a number, and the calling number was not registered on the phone. Cora checked Julia's room on the off chance that she would find a phone book, but there wasn't one. Most likely, Julia had programmed everyone's number into her cell phone, and didn't even have a phone book. Cora went to her own room and crawled into bed still wearing the clothes she had worn to the airport. That was something she didn't usually do—get into bed with her street clothes—she had a real phobia about bringing germs into her bed, but she couldn't do otherwise right now. Cora listened to the silence in the house. She wondered how she would get the details of Charlie's death. She didn't know his folks. Maybe it had already been in the news and wouldn't come up again. She knew she had lost the last few days just spending time with Julia, getting ready for the trip, and ignoring everyone and everything else. Maybe another one of Julia's friends would call. More worrisome to her than getting the details, was the thought of breaking the news to Julia. She considered flying out to Paris so she could be with her daughter when she told her, rather than letting her hear the news on the phone and have to deal with it alone, but she decided against that move. Julia was growing up. She wanted to be out on her own for a while facing the world unaided, Cora thought to herself; she might as well begin handling matters, good, bad, or indifferent, by herself right now. It was all part of becoming an adult. She decided to get out of bed, and rearrange her closet. For goodness sake, it was only twelve minutes after four in the afternoon. She figured that playing around with her clothes would keep her engaged for the next couple of hours; giving her a chance to think. Having a nap now would mean a long sleepless night, and she didn't think she could handle one of those. There was Ambien in her medicine cabinet, but she would really rather not have to pop a pill to get some sleep. Clayton hated the times when Cora told him that she needed a pill to sleep. Always, on the following night he would make sure to be around at bedtime. Usually their lovemaking would soothe her, and after she had fallen asleep, he'd let himself out of the house.

Chapter 15

Clayton Sax, over lunch with one of his colleagues, confided that Cora had once again refused to marry him.

"I asked her again." He began without any kind of prologue, preface, or preamble.

"Asked who, what?"

"I asked Cora to marry me again last night."

"And...?

"And...she refused."

"I'm sorry. I think she's making a mistake."

"Well, thanks. But that's the end of that for me."

"Hmm."

Clayton did not say any more; he swiveled his fork in the spaghetti and shoved a clump of the pale yellow stuff into his mouth. Along with these casual words to his colleague, Clayton also made the decision in his mind that he would not ask Cora to marry him for a fourth time. In fact, he decided that he would start dating other women now. He would not formally dump Cora, nor would he immediately begin pursuing someone else, but he would be open to spending time with other people. He did not plan to fall in love anytime soon, but many women of fine caliber crossed his path, so one never knew what could happen. Cora no longer had to attend every office party on his arm. She did not have to accompany him overseas when he traveled on business. His dating would be without guilt. Cora probably took him for granted, he was thinking. She just sort of *knew* that he would be around, tirelessly waiting, but she needed to think again. It was not that he didn't love her more than he loved anyone in the world, but enough was enough. He had his pride. He could find someone else. He had a lot to bring to someone's table. Cora and he were not going to have a future together. That much was clear to him now.

Riding home in a chauffeur-driven limousine after a long and tense Thursday at work, Clayton thought of traveling to Paris for an extended weekend. He could leave on Saturday morning and stay through Tuesday. Cora had always told him it was the city for curing all the ills that plagued her. He had not visited Paris for that reason in the past, but maybe there was something to the idea. He loved that city anyway, and was familiar with its finest spots, having been there so many times before. Mont Martre was one of his favorite places to hangout. His mind drifted to the Toulouse Lautrec painting of the Moulin Rouge hanging on his kitchen wall. *"Concert BAL Tous Les Soirs,"* he thought to himself. There was a sense of total freedom there; an absence of care, of burden. The artist had captured its spirit well. Summer still lingered, and he could have a good time for a short while. He would let Cora know that he was leaving in case she wanted to send a gift or something to Julia, but she would not be invited to tag along. He immediately pulled his cell phone out of the chest pocket of his jacket, and called his travel agent, Dinah, to have her make the necessary reservations, and then placed a call to Cora from the car. She would have time to drop something off for her daughter on Friday evening if she wanted to do so.

Cora took Clayton's call and noticed with a little flutter in her stomach that instead of an invitation to join him, she was only being given an opportunity to send a gift to her daughter. She always had a bag packed because Clayton was wont to call suddenly to say he was going off on company business for a day or two, and would like her company. She would *always* be invited to tag along. Clayton enjoyed having someone familiar to dine with when he was away from home. It took the edge off his nerves which were usually rattled by all the heavy negotiating and eight-figure deal-making that went on at his business meetings. During the day Cora would explore the area, shop, or avail herself of the hotel's amenities. She would swim, or lounge poolside with a good book. By the time Clayton returned to their room from his business dealings, she would be fresh and relaxed and ready to enjoy his company. For Clayton, being with her was *his* way of relaxing. Very rarely did he schedule a dinner meeting. He liked to spend his evenings with Cora, and wind down after a long day. Cora actually wished he would have dinner meetings because that would mean having his company all day to browse the stores and maybe go sightseeing in the new city, but that was not her decision to make, and she didn't complain. Now she tried to figure out what this change could mean, but decided not to create any bothersome thoughts for herself. There was no point in ruining her night with imaginings. Maybe it meant nothing. Maybe he just had to travel alone this time.

Once at home, Clayton poured himself a double shot of Black Label whiskey, sat down in the burgundy lambskin recliner still fully dressed, and closed his eyes. When he eventually opened them, he glanced at the antique clock on the far wall of the den, and saw that it read 5:15. Several seconds passed before he was able to determine whether it was morning or evening, or what day of the week it was. Backtracking to the actions he remembered last performing, he was able to conclude that it was Friday morning. He bounded up the stairs to the master bedroom, showered, slid into his favorite dark blue Armani suit, and headed back to the office. This time he drove himself there. The green Land Rover was unassuming, but handsomely appointed. He had had himself chauffeured to and from the office all week because he didn't feel like fighting traffic. Sitting in the back seat of a limo, he could read the paper, make a few phone calls, or get work started on his laptop. Today, he would leave home early and drive himself to his office unhurriedly.

Cora decided not to send a gift to her daughter by Clayton. She did not feel like rushing around trying to find just the right thing. There'd be time for that. Julia hadn't left that long ago, anyway. With Clayton out of town this weekend, and without Julia's company either, Cora felt like a fish out of water. She could use a few days of shopping in Aspen. She did volunteer at the local library two days a week reading stories to little ones, but she was sure they'd manage without her for a session or two. Cora volunteered every Wednesday and Thursday after school hours. She chose to do two days together just in case she didn't finish a story on day one. She knew the children would have their parents bring them back the following day to hear the end of it. Kids were like that. She also thoroughly enjoyed spending time with young children. It was her way of giving back. She had had a very privileged childhood, and her parents had left her a nice inheritance. She worked because she needed to do something worthwhile with her time, and needed to socialize. It was why she didn't have one of those crazy nine to five jobs. Instead, she worked with hotels of her choice as a marketing consultant, or sometimes as a member of an advisory board, which meant she made her own hours. She had enough free time to be able to read to kids for an hour or so, twice a week. Volunteering in the middle of the week also allowed her to have extended weekends with Clayton, in or out of town.

Cora called her travel agent to have her book a flight to Colorado, reserve a room at her favorite lodge in Snowmass Village and secure a rental car. She would rather stay in Snowmass Village and do the short drive into Aspen every day, than stay in the glitzy little city her whole trip. She just wanted to shop there. She could easily be cheered up by a little something from Louis Vuitton or Channel, or a piece of jewelry from Judith Ripka. Cora enjoyed spending a lot of money on herself. Skiing she was not into, and it wasn't quite ski season anyway, but the shopping in Aspen was heavenly. She would stay all week. She would give Clayton a chance to figure out what she was up to when he returned to the States and realized that she wasn't at home where he'd left her. It was not exactly payback; she would just call it Even Steven. If traveling alone was good for the gander, it was equally good for the goose.

What Cora would never imagine was that Clayton had visited Julia in Paris even though he had no gift for her from her mother, and therefore no real reason to see her. The visit had been innocent enough on his part; he liked the girl well and felt that she was family, but during that visit Julia had come on to him, and seeing so much of the mother in the girl, he had weakened, and allowed himself to be kissed and caressed by her. He did not encourage Julia's more aggressive advances, or engage in any act of indiscretion with her, but he had let her kiss and caress him for as long as she wanted to. He also made sure that Julia kept all of the action above the waist.

That Tuesday, Clayton returned to the States, and did not know for several days that Cora was out of town. He hadn't tried to contact her. All he could think about was the way Julia had made him feel that evening back in Paris, and how much more of her he wanted, but he reasoned that he was more than three times her age, and pursuing anything with her would just be ridiculous. He would not let himself get carried away by the desires of his own flesh, although he could feel testosterone boiling in his body. Besides the matter of Julia's age, she was Cora's daughter, and he was someone who considered himself a man of great integrity and decency.

Book 3

Chapter 1

Cora pulled the Hertz rental into the driveway of Skier's Haven, went to the VIP Booth and picked up her room key. She never lined up to check in anywhere. She went up to the second floor, entered the suite and was pleased to see that they had given her a room with a fireplace. She always liked a fireplace in her room regardless of the time of year. To her there was something both elegant and comforting about fireplaces. She stripped completely and slipped into the plush white terry robe that hung on the bathroom door. This evening she planned to stay in. She would read, order room service at dinnertime, watch a little television and go to bed. Early tomorrow, after a quick swim and breakfast, she would head out to Aspen. She planned to spend her day milling about, taking in the view, watching celebrity folks, and buying things that caught her fancy. Of course, she would have lunch. There were many nice places to choose from, although she hadn't made her mind up at this point about what exactly she wanted to eat, or where. She realized, as several thoughts crossed her mind, each one for a fleeting moment, that she didn't know the exact day of Clayton's return, but she knew it would be during the time she was away. He had mentioned that he'd be away for "just a few days."

Cora's thoughts turned to Mike—and lingered. When Mike was just a flash in her brain she had neutral feelings about him, and figured she was over the pain of those god-awful experiences she had had with him as her significant other. While she was entangled with him she could have sworn she was having a good relationship. Now, as she looked back? Shit! So when he was a fleeting thought, things were fine. When he lingered on her mind, it was quite a different story. Now Cora felt her hurt and the hate she felt for Mike begin to resurface. She could actually taste the venom in her mouth, felt a sudden desire to spit, but didn't, and felt her throat tighten. She tried to distract herself by flipping through the TV stations using the remote control.

Her thoughts reverted to her relationship with Mike. Throughout her years with him, they had not had sex. He had told her one night that if he had sex with her, he would have to take the relationship to another level and he didn't want to do that. That's the thought that kept coming back to her when she heard that he was marrying a white woman two years after they split up. That's the thought that was plaguing her now, and causing tears to form like crystal pools in her eyes. That was also part of the night drama that she experienced when she lay alone in her bed. Within a year or two of meeting someone new, he had gotten serious enough about that relationship to move it forward and propose marriage. She had hoped that he would love her the way she loved him for all of those six years, but it didn't happen. There were glimmers of love here and there, but they didn't last. They came and went like thunderstorms that arrive without the precursor of lightning; beginning suddenly and being loud enough to make you aware of their presence, then ending without your noticing or knowing which clap of thunder was the last; and then another thunderstorm some months later; same pattern.

During the weeks of grief and distress that followed the news of

Mike's becoming hitched, Cora knew that he had made it clear right from the start and all along the way, by word, if not by deed, that she would not be the one. He had actually spent all their years together verbally pushing her away, but by his actions, he was able to give her enough *something*, call it love, call it hope, call it deception, yes, call it deception, to keep her love; and despite always feeling a partial, sort of low-grade undercurrent of rejection by him, she loved him deeply and chose not to leave. He was always able to eke out just enough promise by something he did to keep her hanging on. Six years down the road, in a phone conversation one Sunday afternoon, he had told her in a rather matter of fact tone when something had come up about her being unhappy:

"I'll tell you the same thing I told you six years ago. If you want to be here, great, if not, you really need to do something else."

The message had been clear in his words and even clearer in his tone. His voice had been almost impatient. Cora knew more certainly than she knew the sun would rise every morning, that this was his way of asking her to leave, like in "How many ways or how many times do I have to tell you to move on?" He sounded urgent about her moving on to find happiness, but she knew it was not about her. It was about his wanting her out of the way so he could pursue someone else. He had fallen in love with a kindergarten teacher, she later learned. Once again, he hadn't had the balls to speak his mind. He wanted it to be all her decision to leave so he would never have to feel guilty about leaving her when all she did was love him unconditionally. He was not man enough to take the responsibility for that, just as he was not man enough to openly date her under the scrutiny of his family, especially the scrutiny of his mother and his brother Hal who always used the N word; That's what Mike told Cora once: that his brother uses the N word.

It was her decision to stay when he told her six years earlier not to ever expect marriage and children, and it had to be her decision now to end the dead-end relationship. He had been pushing her away for years, but that final step had to be hers. That's the way he wanted it. *Then,* he could walk away guiltless; the ballsless son-of-a bitch.

Cora had listened to his words and his tone and had taken it all in stride, and there were several conversations of lighter note over the next few weeks. They continued to talk every day. However, that Sunday's conversation had been the official end of the relationship in her heart. There was no turning back from there. Six years and four hundred thousand shared experiences later, he should not be telling her the same thing he had told her when they first began to date. That day, she decided that she would take herself more seriously, and find the love she knew she deserved.

In her khaki chinos, crisp white button down shirt, and brown croc mules with matching tote, Cora strutted into La Femme, a high-end women's spa in a ritzy part of town, and had her first Brazilian bikini wax. Cora, who now had her thoughts and being under her own constant watch, was amazed that she was totally comfortable letting another woman gently handle her vulva. In fact, she exhaled, tilted her hips forward, and allowed herself to enjoy the experience. The sharp pain she felt as the strip of muslin was yanked from that tender part of her body only served to heighten the thrill. Now, again, Cora paused to monitor her thinking, and clearly established for herself that it was the waxing experience and the idea of doing something new and daring that presented the thrill; not the fact that she was being touched *there* by another woman.

Within three or four weeks of that Sunday's conversation about "doing something else," Mike and Cora talked for the very last time. It was another seemingly calm, pleasant chitchat, but it would be the last time that either of them would contact the other. The next time Cora heard anything about Mike it was two years and three months later, and it was news of his upcoming marriage. The news was broken to her quite inadvertently in a telephone conversation with a past co-worker. The woman she heard it from did not even know that Cora and Mike had been an item. She was just mentioning people that they both knew from an old job, and giving an update on what was going on with them, when there in the midst of everything else was his name and the tidbit of information, and then more news of others of no concern to Cora. Cora thanked God that the news had come that way. She had had a dream about Mike's marrying several days earlier, and this was confirmation. There had always been some kind of intuitive thing between her and Mike. That's why she always knew what he was saying, regardless of the words he actually spoke. He had no doubt communicated with her telepathically about his having moved on and needing to say goodbye forever, hence the dream.

There was no one around to witness Cora's reaction to the news, or hear the screams of hurt that wrenched at her gut when she hung up the phone. Thank goodness. For the next several weeks she would break down in the shower and cry uncontrollably, get teary in the car during her drive to work, and swallow large lumps of emotion that welled up in her throat in the middle of anywhere. Why, she asked God in a tearful fit one day, was she being punished over and over. She had made the same mistakes that other women her age had made; nothing greater; but her whole life seemed to be about paying the price for those mistakes. Youth grants women beauty, but perhaps not wisdom. It seemed to be the case with many people she knew and some she'd only heard of, so why was her punishment so severe?

Cora let herself sink into deep reflection and realized that the life that had seemed so wonderful to onlookers, especially her girlfriends, had really been very difficult, and in many ways demeaning. Things had seemed a lot more glamorous than they were in reality. Sure everyone knew that two members of her family had illnesses that they wrestled with, but these things were minor compared to her own position on the planet. And didn't every family have bad stuff? She had traveled to Europe after high school, and had made the most of her college education there. She kept up a killer body, and landed a great job on her return to the States. By her mid-twenties, she was already managing a chain of luxury hotels—a position that afforded her time and travel to some of the most exotic destinations in the world. To top it off, she was generally admired and liked by everyone she encountered. Then there was the romantic thing she had going with an Adonis of a man who took her out on his yacht for parties, or for lazy pampered weekends. She entertained his friends on the boat, and he showed her the time of her life. A lavish gemstone necklace, or other expensive jewelry was small reward for the envious looks of his buddies or colleagues as they enjoyed his parties, and Mike freely gave them to her. The women Cora knew were either already bored with their marriages to men of mediocre means, divorced, or hoping to meet someone nice; nice like her Mike, meaning rich, tall, good-looking, world's greatest legs, and generous. Those gorgeous features and mop of jet-black hair were stunning above his six-foot-two frame. Actually, he was six foot three, and carried his height well. They knew nothing of the anguish that nestled in Cora's heart, or the diminished sense of self she felt when she returned from these weekend jaunts with her beau. She mentioned to him once, that somehow these weekend jaunts made her feel more disconnected from him, and she didn't understand why. He had said nothing in response. He usually didn't indulge in conversations of that nature, either because he had no idea what she was talking about, or just refused to go there with her; and then she had to consider the man factor. Men had a way of never discussing emotions. Cora could never decide if they just didn't feel things in the same way that women did, or if they just had no words to describe their feelings. Whatever the reason, it was the rare man who could talk about feelings or share emotions at all. Maybe men vented by constantly clicking the remote control, and screaming at their TV screens during ball games. She didn't know. Of course, that inability to converse about these matters left her feeling more frustrated than ever, and after a while she gave up making even the slightest effort at conversing along those lines. They discussed information gathered by the five senses with no interpretation of anything heard or seen. Things touched, smelled, and tasted gave them a little more leeway in terms of conversation; smooth was smooth, flowery was flowery—maybe, and salty was salty; they could agree on most of that and elaborate.

Only Cora Jenkins knew that her self-esteem was gradually slipping away, gradually being eroded, and many were the nights she lay awake wondering what would make Mike love her the way she wanted to be loved by him. It was not so much about his decision not to marry her, but more about the way he made her feel not good enough. It was beginning to occur to her that contrary to the belief of some people, love *did* know color. She wished that Mike would stick up for her, be proud of her, and treasure her. She no doubt felt the racist sting when initially Mike's guests on the boat, caucasian like himself, had thought she was the help and had smiled at her condescendingly, with barely a thank you when she served them a drink. There were the vacations at the Cape and at the Vineyard where white people had stared at her, then at him, and then back at her with disgust written all over their faces. Mike had been oblivious to it all. Strangers would engage him in conversation while waiting on line at the bank or at the airport, and never glance her way even once to include her in the conversation. Cora had not been able to communicate these things to Mike because he hadn't noticed anything, and would certainly think it was all in her mind. Even the things he *did* see did not make an impression on him one way or the other, or so he said. Or maybe they did make an impression, and furthered his resolve to keep her from being in his life in any significant way. If anything was ever mentioned, his reasoning was that the offender had probably just had a moment of thoughtlessness. He thought that most people were a little weird, anyway. Maybe she was just being self conscious. (After all, this was the 21st century, and all of that segregation and prejudice has been done away with. Of course, this change has not yet registered in the minds or experiences of black people, Mike was thinking). Cora knew better. She thought life in America was very much like life on George Orwell's Animal Farm where all animals were equal, but some were more equal than others. Worst of all, she suspected that he harbored the same prejudices and was fighting to suppress them, making believe they existed only in the hearts of his family members, and not in his. It was because of the family's prejudice and negative feelings about Blacks that he could not invite her to the family gatherings. That's what he said, and hoped she would believe it. Maybe that's what he believed himself.

Cora thought now about how Mike would meet his relatives for dinner alone, and get away as soon as he could to come by and see her, before scooting off again. He'd call from her house to tell his folks that he'd had a good time, but had stopped by a friend for a visit, and would talk to them when he got home later.

One day Cora got up the nerve to tell her man that although he blamed the racist attitudes on his parents and brother, Hal (his biggest excuse for not taking her home to meet them), the problem was really his. He shifted his embarassed eyes from her direct gaze, and hung his head in silence, his face turning pink; not the rosy pink of a prideful blush, but rather the purplish pink of guilt and shame, and after failing to respond verbally for several, several seconds, she had changed the topic to relieve his obvious discomfort. That particular topic never came up again.

Channel 7. Good! The news was on. Maybe there was something interesting going on in the world. She watched for a while, and no story was of that much interest to her until she saw the news report about a famous black actor who was receiving hate mail and death threats in New York because he was married to a white woman. No one thus far could trace the origin of the mail, but the actor had received three letters already, and there was also a threat of burning down a store where his white and also famous wife had been seen shopping.

Cora felt her face flush with heat and then instantly chill with a cold sweat. She slid out of the robe and back into her sweater and jeans. Getting back into underwear would have taken her a few more seconds. She didn't have time. She needed to act, like yesterday. The cashmere jeans felt soft against her nude body, and for a moment she had an all-over feeling of sensuousness, but that was fleeting. Throwing her pocket book carelessly over her left shoulder, she walked to the elevator bank and hit the down button three times to hurry the elevator's arrival on her floor. It came. She got in, pressed *Lobby*, felt one swift drop down, got out of the once-again-open elevator door, walked quickly to the hotel parking lot, found her car, got in, turned the key in the ignition, and revved out of the parking lot at top speed. She seemed to be on autopilot now, and she had no time to lose. Cora realized as she was speeding away that she hadn't even checked for any other traffic or vehicles around her, but so far so good. She hadn't hit anyone or even had a close call. She drove into Aspen and quickly found a pay phone—a rare find in that city, since everyone was glued to a cell phone or BlackBerry. She exited the car and slammed the door shut. The noise of the door slamming startled her as though she hadn't expected it. Cora's heart raced. She seemed strangely aware of every pulse point in her body and felt the throbbing of each one. All the beats were synchronized, but she felt each one separately. There was the flush of heat and then immediate chill to her face again. She entered the phone booth and dialed the number for the anonymous tips criminal hotline in New York. She told the voice that answered the phone that she had just watched a chilling news story about the extent to which some people would take their bigotry, and knew for sure who had sent the letters to the actor. He was locally known as a hater of Blacks and other minorities, and had always talked of bringing one of them down for thinking that monetary success and a public face could make any of them worthy of marrying into the white race. She asked for the detective in charge. She was asked to hold. When another man came on the line and identified himself as Officer Donahue, the chief detective, Cora gave Mike's name as the perpetrator of the crime, furnished his address, and quickly hung up the phone. The police could probably trace the call, but she would be nowhere around. That's the reason she had driven away from the hotel to find a pay phone.

Driving back to the lodge, Cora could feel the rush of blood to her face, and her heart pounding heavily beneath her sweater. Her fingertips were ice cold, and her knees felt a little weak. She eased her right foot off the gas and took a deep breath in an effort to slow down her brain, slow the car down, and calm herself. She was sure that Mike would not be found guilty if these allegations resulted in a trial. He would definitely have alibis for every time that he was accused of doing this dirty little act. He was a creature of habit and routine, and very calculating in his actions. He would not have spontaneously gone off on a trip or anything like that, so of course the police could pick him up for questioning, and he would know exactly where he was, who he was with, and what he was doing on every day, at every hour. There were no mindless actions in his life. He would be able to prove everything he told the police and other legal authorities, and would eventually get out of the predicament. However, the allegations would rattle his nerves, cause the psoriasis patches to break out on his elbows and belly again, and he would have the trouble and the expense of hiring a lawyer and going through the courts to clear his name. Forever after that, his friends would question whether or not there was some truth to the accusations. He would wonder if his mother felt the same about him now that he had gotten entangled with the police. He was, after all, the good son. Co-workers would talk. He would always and forever be uneasy among the people he always wanted so much to impress. His life would never be the same again. *Son of a Bitch!* Cora was sure that Mike had breathed a sigh of relief when she left him without question or confrontation. She knew he felt blessed to have the gods in his favor though he never went to church, and was for the most part agnostic. She hoped now, that he was smart enough to know there was no such thing as an easy escape, or a clean getaway. *Son-of-a Bitch!* Over the years she'd watched him grow into an arrogant something, full of himself, and bent on making her believe he was superior to her. Intellectually she knew better. She was teaching him things on a daily basis; simple things like table manners, and complex things like how the United Nations worked. "What exactly was the General Assembly?" he had asked. She had explained in detail and after several very dumb questions, he seemed to get it. Yet in her heart she felt less than he. Cora remembered her first visit to his studio apartment in a luxury complex, and how amazed she was that a six-foot-two or three-inch man could sleep on a twin size bed jammed into a corner of the room. Everything there had been filthy. The pale blue sheets had turned a dingy brown, and his towels did not drape themselves over a bar. Instead, they stood like dirty sculptures behind the door; literally holding themselves up without assistance. She had gone out and bought him a new set of rich burgundy colored sheets of a high thread count. She could see them now. She replaced the towels which had never been washed, and coaxed him into buying at least a queen size bed. By the time they split up, he had bought a house in a nice section of town, and was well on his way to becoming a person. It was amazing how he managed to make her feel that she was somehow beneath him. Right before the breakup he had asked her to move in with him, but couldn't tell her how he planned to handle his parents' coming to visit, which was something she asked about, knowing that his biggest effort in life was made at hiding her from his family. He had hidden her once before at a public function, and she knew that her pictures went into the trunk under his bed when his friends came to visit. Very many years had passed since there was anything between them, but Cora knew every detail of Mike's life and whereabouts. From a distance she had kept her finger on his pulse; had made it her duty to do so. Every now and then she would check in with mutual friends of theirs and innocently pose her questions, making sure never to let too much enthusiasm for the information show in her voice.

Cora finally got back to her room at the lodge, surprised that she had done so without getting into an accident on her way to or from that pay phone, and after taking a quick hot shower, climbed into bed and slept like a baby.

The next morning she felt as calm as if nothing had happened the night before. She walked to the sofa, slid deep down into the plush upholstery, put her feet on the coffee table and admired the majesty of the mountains through the open window. Here in Colorado the mountains loomed so close you felt you could reach out and touch them. Cora regarded these mountains as proof that God was majestic and divine in the way he had ordered the world. She also thought that being given the opportunity to screw Mike over was further proof of the divine order of things. The son-of-a-bitch would be in such deep doo-doo. Nothing in life was without a reason, be it pleasure or pain. First came one, then the other and then both started all over again. She knew that without either one there could never be true understanding of, or appreciation for the other, and that both served the higher purpose of the soul. She had read Zukov and Chopra and Dyer and Carlos Casteneda. They were her favorite authors. They understood. They were the masters. She was the student. She tried to understand, and at times felt that she was getting there. However, she found that while she studied and waited to reach their level of enlightenment, some banal earth matters needed to be taken care of here and now, and she was both willing and able to take care of them in a way that she thought fair. Cora was big on fairness. Tomorrow she would suspend judgment of her fellow man and see the connection between herself and all that dwells on the planet. Today Mike needed his arse fixed for his freshness and disrespect. What in hell made him think that he was superior to her? The color of his skin? He was less educated than she was despite having degrees that were equivalent to hers in name. Cora was very much aware of the thick line between education and academic achievement. In fact, she thought a brick wall, rather than a line divided the two. Anyone could obtain a degree if he or she stayed in school long enough and doggedly pursued some specific course work. Education, on the other hand, was an enlightened state of mind; consciousness. It rendered one experienced, open-minded, accepting of others, knowledgeable about how things worked with money, with politics, with government, with addictions, with human nature, with various perspectives and norms, with customs and mores in a vast number of societies. The son of a bitch wasn't close to being educated. He ate chicken with broccoli from the Chinese restaurant near his job every day, and then ordered it in for dinner at night, like there was no other food in the world. When he thought he was being adventurous, for example, when he dined out with her, he would have Mahi Mahi. He took vacations only in the Caribbean; one or two islands. While there, he never mingled with the native people. Throughout his stay he would go from his hotel room to the beach to the pool to his room and start all over again until he was ready to go to the airport and take the trip back home. He said that he had no interest in Europe(where his ancestors were from), or Africa or any other continent. He called those seven visits to Barbados, and one each to two other Caribbean islands, "having traveled so much now." Cora thought that ants covered more ground going up and down a pole in a straight line. The other thing about Mike that pissed Cora off big-time was his belief in the editorials he read in the newspaper, or listened to on the radio, or watched on television. If they said it on TV, it had to be true as far as he was concerned. Naïve!! He never grasped the concept that an editorial was usually presented with the editor's personal slant. Cora remembered how Mike had struggled to use his knife and fork correctly, and she remembered the time at a beach party at a fancy resort when he attempted to take his used plate back to the buffet table for a refill. She had quickly snatched it out of his hand and saved him the embarrassment. As he shoveled in his second helping, she noticed that he held his fork like a weapon, stabbing at every morsel he wanted to put into his mouth. Yet he looked down on her brown skin and deemed himself better than she was. The nerve! If anyone should deem himself better than another, Cora thought, it should be based on values, decorum, humaneness, integrity, education, breeding and the like; not on the hue of the epidermis—the shallowest of all measures. Just right below that thin brown or cream layer of skin, things were darned near identical, in terms of composition. Then there were the aspects of being that had nothing to do with the physical appearance. Didn't the asshole son of a bitch know that?

A knock on the door brought Cora's mind back from its meanderings to her immediate surroundings. She pulled the two sides of the white terry cloth robe together, knotted the belt to make sure she was completely covered, and hurried to the door in her bare feet.

"Hello?"

"Housekeeping."

Cora moved the chain on the door and opened it just wide enough to show her face and middle part of her body.

"Good Morning. Housekeeping."

"I'll just exchange my towels for a fresh set," Cora told the pretty Mexican lady standing there with her cleaning cart fully loaded.

"Are you sure, Ma'am?"

"Oh, yes. I didn't make much of a mess. Thanks." Cora said with a pleasant smile. She now opened the door fully.

"Okay. Here you go. Thank you."

Cora was handed a stack of bath towels, face towels, and washcloths; two of each she guessed.

"Thanks so much. Have a good day," she said closing the door with her right hand and balancing the stack of towels on an open left palm.

The woman smiled and showed two rows of perfectly lined up yellowish teeth. The first ones of that color Cora had seen in a while since everyone she knew had already put their teeth through the magic whitening process that had become so suddenly popular and chic. She knew from her travels to many countries and exposure to many cultures, that none were as vain as her fellow Americans. Hers was a nation obsessed with appearances: looks, titles, symbols of affluence, social associations, you name it.

Cora thanked the woman once again, closed the door and returned to the couch laying the towels down beside her. The room could be left undone for another day, she thought half to herself, half out loud. She felt that she urgently needed to get back to her thoughts. She was already picturing Mike's face as he answered the knock on his front door, and stared in consternation as the designated spokesperson of the group of four policemen told him that he needed to come down to the stationhouse for questioning. She saw his wife's gaze of disbelief as she wondered if she really knew the man she'd married. After all, she'd only known him a little over two years when they pledged their lives and love to each other. Cora heard Mike's voice saying that he was willing to come to the precinct and cooperate fully with the investigation, and that handcuffs would not be necessary. In fact, she heard him volunteer to drive himself to the precinct, his voice tremulous and cracking, but the policemen were not going for that. They had their own way of doing things. Who was this guy, anyway? And why should they change their procedures for him? Cora read Mike's thoughts, and knew that he would be thinking of his mother now. Would this event be the one to send her to her grave, and not his bringing home a black woman after all? The smile that crossed Cora's face and lingered on her lips made her eyes squint and her nostrils flare. Who gets to strut their ass in arrogance now? She who struts last, struts best, Cora was thinking; never mind laughing last; strutting took the cake. In fact, strutting, like Mirandy and Ezel in "Mirandy and Brother Wind" was bound to win the cakewalk. Yes, Mike was a son-of-a-bitch all right, and deserved nothing less than a life distressed; his paradise lost. Cora's plan for revenge, though not yet fully brought to fruition, already tasted oh so sweet.

Chapter 2

Julia, in the meantime, was enjoying Paris. Like her mother, shopping was one of her favorite things to do and she found that Place Vendome was a good spot for her to do that. She visited and shopped there every other day, or so. The problem was that Julia was not engaged in any meaningful activity. She was not in school, and didn't have a job, and knew that after a while she would become bored out of her mind, and broke. At the point when she came to Paris, she was close to graduation back at home, but that was not going to happen now; maybe it wouldn't happen until the novelty of Paris and being on her own had worn off. She was close to her eighteenth birthday already, so maybe by the time she was ready to get back to her studies, she would have to settle for a G.E.D. She had taken all of her savings with her, thanks to her mother's generosity, but money was a finite commodity, and she knew it. Maybe she would get herself back to the United States if, or when, she grew sick of Paris. She didn't have to let her mother know she was returning home. She could go to San Francisco and find a job, maybe meeting and greeting guests at one of the swankier hotels. It was a great, hip city with a live-and let-live attitude. The men there might be of a different sexual preference than she was used to, but at this point, considering her rape and all, that would be okay with her. She would work in San Francisco from Monday to Friday, and go off to Sausalito every weekend. She liked the beauty and affluence of that place, and it was the San Franciscans' favorite place to hang out. Monterey would be her weekend option if she wanted to shop. A girl needed to shop. She could picture herself living like that for a while; for a very long while.

These thoughts Julia was having on a Tuesday morning around eleven o'clock. When Clayton phoned her from the States on Wednesday around noon to say that he'd had a nice visit with her in Paris, she asked him to send her some money because she was running low on cash and didn't want to bother Cora. She promised that she would pay the money back as soon as she found a job. She had been job-hunting every day for the last few weeks, and was sure something was going to come up for her very soon. Of course, she would not be able to refund all of the money at once, but would start paying it back with her very first paycheck, and every time she got paid she would repay as much as she could afford. Clayton completely bought that bag of lies that Julia disguised as genuine promises and immediately agreed to wire her five thousand dollars. He knew that Paris was an expensive city to live in, and Julia was used to having as much spending money as she needed or wanted from Cora. He copied her account and bank information on a post-it pad that was lying on his desk, ripped the page out, and stuck it in the breast pocket of his jacket. Julia used a Citibank in Paris. That made things easy. He banked with Citibank in the States. It was not an exorbitant sum of money for a short-term loan, he reasoned, and he was sure something would come up for her soon.

In actuality, something did come up for Julia. It was the penis in Clayton's pants; so that by the time he got to his bank and transferred the money into Julia's account, he had increased the amount to ten thousand dollars, and decided he would tell her the next time they spoke, that she didn't have to pay the money back.

Chapter 3

Back at a Brooklyn Precinct, Mike was sweating his ass off trying to remember where he was at the time of those hate crimes and threats that the police were now trying to pin on him. As his lack of luck would have it, the investigator turned out to be a black cop. Given the issue he was being questioned about, Mike sort of knew that his ass was grass, to coin a phrase. Once again he found himself praying to the God he wasn't sure existed. He had done this exercise in prayer only one other time in his life—when his mother was put on dialysis, and he wasn't sure she'd make it.

If a white cop had been assigned to this investigation, things might have been a little easier for him, Mike was thinking, but maybe the next man for handling the newly arrested was this black guy. God help him!

"So what do you know about these threats?" The policeman asked without any pleasantries.

"Exactly what threats are you referring to?"

"The. threats. to. the. black .movie. star. in. which. you. promised. to. kill. him."

"I have no idea what you're talking about.

"What do you mean you have no idea? Let me break it *down*. It was all over the fucking news, chump."

"I don't know. I didn't threaten anyone."

"What about burning down the store where his *wife* was shopping?"

"You got me. I have no idea."

"Damn *right* I got you! You fucking idiot! Talk to me! Or should I *kick* the information out of you?"

"Hey bud, come here," the officer said, signaling with a quick movement of an open left palm to another black cop.

"What's going on?" asked the arriving colleague as he walked toward the two men

"This is the idiot we brought in for those death threats to the brother. He says he has no idea what threats we're talking about."

Mike noticed that this new officer wore a couple more pins on his uniform and didn't think that was a good omen; not for him in his current predicament; not with hate crimes hanging over his head. Hadn't he heard a spokesperson for the One Hundred Blacks in Law Enforcement say there wasn't enough of them? So far, he was stuck with two. He continued to sit motionless, alternating his gaze between one man and the other.

The newly arrived officer walked over to the table where the two men sat, pulled a chair up alongside Mike, lined his mouth up with Mike's left ear, and spoke directly into it(Mike was now thinking *Neurological Impress*; a strategy for teaching kids to read).

"You got a problem with ebony brothas bein' with sistas from the Milky Way?"

"Nope. People are people, you know?"

"Oh, I know! Do **YOU** fuckin' know? **ANSWER ME!**"

Jumping out of his skin at the sound of the booming voice in his ear and the big black fist coming down on the table in front of them, Mike replied:

"Why did you pick me? I didn't do anything. I wasn't even in town during the time you're talking about."

"Oh, no? You had a KKK meetin' somewhere? **ANSWER ME!**"

Another boom into his left ear and another big bang on the table made Mike stand up suddenly and put his hands on his hips. A smirk crossed the lips of the first investigator who was sitting across the table from his colleague and Mike.

"**SIT DOWN!** We're not done here. Got an alibi?"

Mike sat down abruptly and let his hands drop between his knees.

"Actually, yes. My mother was with me. I had taken her to visit her sister in Connecticut during the time you're referring to."

"Your **motha**? Your **motha** can't be your alibi. Do **you** think that **I** think she's gonna tell the truth? Do I look like a fuckin' idiot to you?"

"I'm just telling you, man."

"**Man?** I'm the Deputy Chief of Police! See here?" (pointing to his badge).

"I'll ask you again: Do you think I look like a *fucking* idiot?"

Mike thought to himself that the **g** at the end of that last **fucking** was a surprise, but only answered:

"No."

"Do all black people look like *fucking idiots* to you?"

Another **g** at the end of **fucking**, Mike noted.

"No."

"Then who's the fucking idiot, you? Because somebody's gotta be a *fucking* idiot."

At that point, Mike decided he had better stop trying to answer the policeman's questions and call somebody with that one phone call he initially didn't think he needed. There was no way he could give any answers to this guy that would be deemed correct or appropriate. He was sure that his mother knew someone. His uncle had been a hot-shot lawyer. He wished he could summon his help from the grave. He wished he knew how he had gotten into this mess to begin with. He had no clue under the sun how he got pulled into the station for questioning about a matter he was totally innocent about. Was it someone's idea of a joke? His friend Ashton was an outrageous practical joker, but this situation was really getting out of hand, as far as Mike was concerned.

"Can I make a phone call?"

"Sure. Use my cell phone."

The officer removed his cell phone from his shirt pocket and placed it on the table between them.

"Can I use the station phone?" Mike did not carry a cell phone. He always thought it was completely unnecessary, and way too small to play around with.

"USE **MY** CELL PHONE."

Another loud bang as the cell phone was picked up by the officer and this time slammed down on the table, resulted in another big jump out of the skin by Mike. For a moment he felt like he was losing his mind. Taking the cell phone while shifting his eyes back and forth between the two policemen again, Mike tried to decide whether to call his mother, or his wife, to have one of them find him a lawyer. The officer who had begun the interrogation had been totally silent for the last several minutes, leaving him at the mercy of the Deputy Chief, who seemed to be some kind of raving lunatic. What Mike was also thinking, but didn't dare utter, was that a big, black, loud man with a dark blue uniform and bright, white teeth could scare the crap out of the very God who had created him. He imagined that God must at this moment feel a kinship with Mary Shelley and must be thinking those famous words from *Frankenstein*: I beheld the wretch, the miserable monster that I created. Or something like that. Mike hoped that God was on his side, he being now also afraid of the deputy chief, his own creation.

Mom got the vote. Mike decided that he would call his mother. She was better connected than his wife. He dialed the number and let it ring twenty-one times. No one answered the phone. His mother had no answering machine. It was one of those new things that she didn't think she needed. In her day, when you called someone and they were not at home, you called back later.

"My mother's not home," said Mike sheepishly. "I have to call someone else."

"**ONE** phone call, Brotha. You should've got it right the first time. It's 9 P.M. Don't you know where your mommy is?"

Mike exhaled and resigned himself to spending the night in jail. This crazy guy had just called him brother. He had always thought that black men only called other black men brother. Maybe the rules had changed. Who knew how this shit worked! The other day he saw the new black president giving a bear hug to some white Congress guy on the news. "It's a brave, new world." Mike thought. Maybe tomorrow this fog would clear. Maybe he would wake up and discover that he had dreamt the whole thing, though something in his gut told him it was all very real, and that his heavenly life had just walked right through the widely yawning mouth of Hell.

Chapter 4

Cora returned from Aspen, and decided to put a call in to Julia. Would she break the news of Charlie's death now, or had the girl already found out somehow? Would she have to gauge her mood, and then decide? Cora thought she might as well make the call. Maybe Julia already knew. It would be easier that way. She swallowed hard and dialed the fifteen numbers that would get her daughter on the line; get this over and done with. After two rings, there was Julia's voice. She sounded calm.

"Hello."

"Hi Julia, it's Mom."

"Oh, Hi. How come you didn't call to tell me Charlie died?"

"I was just..."

"I just happened to call Pam, and she blurted out that she was sorry. When I asked her what about, she said Charlie. Then she told me that he'd shot himself."

"Yes. When I got home from taking you to the airport there was a message from Pam. I didn't have the details at first, but then several of your friends called the house looking for you, and gradually the story unfolded..."

"Oh, well." Julia said complacently. "I guess he couldn't live with himself anymore."

"What makes you say that, Julia? I thought you loved him. I expected you to be all upset."

"Yeah, I'm upset, but not about his death."

"I don't understand."

"No, you don't! What have you been up to?" Julia asked, quickly changing the subject. "Where have you been? I tried calling you at the house the other day. I didn't bother trying your cell phone."

"I was probably just out. Why didn't you leave a message?"

"No reason."

Cora knew by the dead silence that followed that short answer that Julia was ready to get off the phone, and would not be talking about Charlie, or her whereabouts in Paris, or anything else, but pressed on:

"So, Julia, how are you? What's going on with you?"

"Nothing new; nothing to report, really. I'm kinda tired.

"Okay. Well, relax. Be well. Everything's okay on this side. If you need anything, call. I'm here."

"Thanks. Chat soon."

"Bye."

Cora held the phone to her ear for a moment longer but there was nothing more from Julia's end, except the click of the phone as the receiver was dropped into the cradle. She slowly put her own receiver down.

That evening, Cora brooded over the thought that Julia seemed a very different person from the one she saw off at the airport not so long ago. Did she see that coming? It hit her that not once during the conversation with her daughter had Julia used the word Mom. She usually called her Mom. At times in the past, when Julia was being playful, she would even call her mother by her first name. That didn't happen either. Cora had tons of questions that she wanted answered about how Julia was doing in Paris. Had she looked around for a school? Had she contacted any of the numbers in Paris that Cora had her take with her? Was she happy being away from home? Did she even miss her mother? All she knew was that Julia was not talking tonight, and her questions would have to wait. Her mind shifted back to the devious little deed she'd done in Aspen, and she wondered how she would find out how Mike had fared in the mess that she had thrown him into. She picked up the receiver, and dialed Alison's number. There was no answer. She hung up and dialed Charlotte's number. Cora had not been in touch with either of these girls in a little while, but they both were in some singing group with Mike. She figured one of them would have gotten wind of his little saga by now.

Chapter 5

Mike's wife, his mother, and their attorney friend, Howard Williamson, arrived at Mike's cell early the next morning, just in time to hear three other prisoners chiding him about "looking too cute to hang out in a joint like this." He had been sitting on the bench, purple in the face, looking down at his shoes and trying not to respond to their taunts. One of the men was saying that at least this place guaranteed him three hots and a cot. Mike figured that meant three hot meals and a bed to sleep in, but he wasn't quite sure. He guessed it was street language of some sort; maybe it had nothing to do with eating and sleeping, so he let that slide, too.

At the sound of his fellow inmates beginning to cheer, Mike looked up and was relieved to see his friend, his mother, and his wife. He suddenly felt very hopeful that his nightmare was about to end. At least they could post bail and get him out of that hellhole. He thought of repeat offenders, and wondered what they were thinking, committing crime after crime after crime and returning to a place like this.

The attorney got to work immediately and requested that Mike be released without bail on his own recognizance, but the request was denied. Mike would probably be able to go home to his family tomorrow after he'd been formally charged, and could stay out of jail pending the trial. They would also require bond money of two hundred thousand dollars. Had there been an actual attempt at murder, Mike would be looking at a million dollars in bond money, or would, worse yet, be held without bail, but there had only been nasty letters. There had also been a threat of arson. The authorities could not let him just walk out of the place; neither did they have any other suspects. The police had acted on their one and only lead.

Tomorrow came and Mike was charged with three counts of harassment with a threat to commit murder, and one count of a threat to commit arson. Bail was posted by the lawyer, since he was a long-time family friend, and Mike went home with his wife. The attorney would take his mother home and call her doctor. In the space of one day, she had become so pale and gaunt that he thought she should have immediate medical attention. She already had not been feeling well, but put off calling her doctor when she heard the news of Mike's arrest which made her deathly ill, in order to accompany her daughter-in-law to her son's cell.

Mike spent the next few weeks at home in his pajamas, just going in and out of the bathroom. He lost everything he ate, either through his mouth or through his backside. The few moments he had between visits to the bathroom were spent mopping beads of sweat from his forehead and armpits. His wife decided to sleep in another bedroom because he tossed and turned all night, and had such a stench about his person from not having showered in days, that she couldn't catch her breath. She suggested her husband see his doctor, but he was afraid to leave the house. If he so much as heard a police or ambulance siren in the neighborhood, he covered his face and cowered in fear. His mother came to the house and offered to give him a bath in bed and put some ointment on the psoriasis patches that had spread like wildfire all over his stomach, but he refused her help. So Mike continued to reside in the master bedroom, duck under the covers every time he heard a loud noise, lose every meal he ate, and stink to high heaven.

His wife prayed for strength during this trying time, but knew that if this situation kept up the way it was going now, she'd be forced to leave him. It didn't matter that he had been eager to marry her, or that his relatives had embraced her as though she were born into their own family. Was she in love with him when they married? Yes and no. They got along well and she liked him a lot, but mostly it was about nabbing someone she could rely on to share financial responsibility. The same went for him. Besides, she was already thirty-six, and needed to find a husband. She also thought there was little likelihood of his being unfaithful, so overall he was a good catch. She'd be silly to let him slip through her fingers, the way his ex had. It didn't take genius to recognize when someone else's loss was your gain. At least, that's what she thought at the time she said "*I do.*"

Chapter 6

Gilbert's death had in an unexpected way drawn Ken and Thelma together. Ken found himself seeking Thelma out and talking to her about his feelings on several occasions; sharing more of his feelings than he had really planned to. Thelma was amazed that she had not been unwilling to talk to Ken. He would knock on the door of her cabin, and she would come out to say hello. Realizing that hello was turning into a conversation, they would go up to the deck and sit for a while, chatting as the ship sailed along. Sometimes two hours would go by before one of them decided it was time to go do something else. Usually, Ken did most of the talking and Thelma listened with the appropriate interjections from time to time. She found him interesting, and actually enjoyed his company. Thelma noted to herself that enjoying people's company was not customary for her, but it was something she could get used to. With Gilbert off the boat, everyday life for her was less tense; things were generally a little easier. She didn't have to loathe getting near the captain to take orders, or watch with disgust as he enjoyed the company of his lover and guests, while she felt that eternal emptiness in the pit of her stomach and waited for another chance to end his life.

By and by, a conversation came up between the two about love and marriage, and Ken began a story about a young black woman he had once been quite smitten by, but he had already known that he was gay, and thought it best not to begin a romantic relationship with her. She, on the other hand, considered him her man. The two had been great friends, though, and one night they did make love, quite by happenstance. It had been the first and only time they'd been together that way. After the incident, he had decided that the best course of action was to get out of her life altogether. He thought she deserved better than a complicated ambivalent relationship.

Ken gazed into the distance as he said, partly to Thelma, partly to himself: "She was a great gal. We met in Paris. I actually really loved her. Her name was Cora. Cora Jenkins."

Ken's eyes returned to Thelma just in time to see her body involuntarily shudder. He also saw her swallow hard, which made him think she was having some romantic flashback of her own. He didn't ask her to tell him about it. He thought that his openness with her would eventually encourage her to share her own stories. He could wait. He thought that she, too, was an interesting character, and believed that one day he would find out what really made her tick.

Thelma felt her heart thumping as if it would beat itself right out of her chest, but did not give any indication to Ken that his story had registered with her on any level. She hoped that he hadn't caught the shudder. She immediately began to think, however, that maybe the same set of circumstances had transpired between Ken and her daughter, Cora, as had happened between Gilbert and herself all those years earlier. Life had a strange way of rerunning scenarios as though they were rehearsals of acts in a play. Had Cora also given birth to a baby daughter? If she had, then Thelma hoped at least, that Cora was able to keep her. For the first time in a long time, she was aware of an emotion other than hate, disgust, or total indifference. Thelma became aware of a feeling of love for her daughter and whatever offspring she might have had. She wished that her own life had turned out differently. Thelma thought that her life could probably have been close to normal despite having to put her daughter up for adoption, were it not for the spate of nervous breakdowns that followed as a result of all she had gone through. Her mental illness had been the undoing of her hopes and ambitions. She had always dreamed that Cora would create a loving family for herself, and have the family life that she, Thelma, never could, but now with this new story out of Ken's mouth, the dream suddenly seemed to be slipping away. She began to toy with the idea of murdering Ken for creating a situation that could potentially have ruined her daughter's life, the way her own had been ruined by Gilbert. She would have to give the whole thing further thought. Maybe everything *was* okay with her daughter. Why should she imagine the worst? But there was a sinking feeling in her stomach that she couldn't shake. She was hoping that with Gilbert gone, she could finally release her feelings of anger and need for revenge, and probably move toward a peaceful existence, if nothing else, but now she wondered if that, too, was another empty dream.

Over the next few days, Thelma did everything in her power to avoid contact or direct conversation with Ken. She didn't want anything he did or said to influence her thinking about him one way or the other. She needed to make a clearly thought-out decision about whether he continued to live, or die at her behest. She had always harbored a modicum of resentment for Ken because he was able to creep into Gilbert's heart in a way she hadn't been able to, but she hadn't considered taking his life. Thelma remembered the feeling that arose in her chest the moment she realized what was going on between the two men. Two balls of lead seemed to come from nowhere and lodge themselves in the middle of her rib cage. A third one lodged itself in her throat, and the whole upper area of her body felt a dull, heavy pain. The leaden balls were cold and gray, and sat firmly in those spaces. She took stock of the resentment she felt for Ken because he seemed to have won a place in Gilbert's heart that he, Gilbert, had never even thought about offering to her. She noted that beyond the resentment for Ken, she felt unbridled hatred for Gilbert, and the two sentiments were separate and distinct in her heart. At times her resentment for Ken would dissipate, if only to resurface at another time, but the hatred she felt for Gilbert was constant and immovable. Its presence was always with her as the main character in that movie she called her life, and everything else played second fiddle to it. Prior to Gilbert's suicide, Thelma had spent every waking moment of every day envisioning and planning various ways of bringing about his demise; hence her relief when he did it himself. Feelings about Ken had not been as strong, until tonight. Now, indeed, Thelma thought, God and Karmic laws took care of some matters, but there were other matters that had to be handled by humans here on earth, and in near future time, if not immediately. She was glad that she had kept the gun, and not thrown it overboard after Gilbert was gone. That thought had crossed her mind. Maybe she should first find out where and how her Cora was, but she felt certain that her daughter's life had been a replay of hers, and wanted to work from that knowledge. She didn't think Ken would know any more than he'd already told, and she didn't know what else to think.

Chapter 7

In Paris, Citibank called to notify Julia that funds had been wired from overseas to her account, and that they were available at her local branch whenever she was ready to collect them. She hung up the phone and promptly made her way to her Citibank which happened to be three or four blocks away. She was not the least bit surprised to find that ten thousand dollars had been wired to her account instead of the agreed-upon five. She knew that Clayton had been surprised by her advances. Maybe he had been smitten, too. She figured that he had been attracted to or by her, and that only his integrity and maybe some consideration for her mother, had prevented him from giving in to his feelings for her. She would withdraw two thousand dollars now to cover her rent, utilities, and the new Coach pocket book. No need to spend it all in one day, though the dress shops at La Place Vendome had been calling her name.

The bank teller who waited on Julia was a handsome young man; real G.Q. cover type, Julia thought to herself as she slipped her bank card under the slot at his window and told him how much she wanted to withdraw. The young gentleman appeared to be in his mid-twenties, clean-cut and intelligent looking. Julia had eyed him every few seconds while she waited her turn on line. She had hoped that she would get to go to his window. She did. The young fellow seemed immediately taken with her, and tried to make small talk in between updating her account and counting out the money she requested. After shuffling around a bit, he found an envelope in which to put the withdrawn funds and scribbled his name, James, and a phone number on it. Directly beneath the phone number, in shakier handwriting, he wrote the words: "Call me." He didn't remember whether or not there was a rule for bank employees against doing that sort of thing, and he didn't think the girl would report him, if there were. Most women would see that as flattering and would at worst ignore it if they didn't have any interest in the guy. They weren't about to run to the authorities about something like that. He would take his chances. He knew he'd remember her name, and could access her personal information from the bank files, but he thought that giving her his own name and number was less risky business.

"Call me later?" James said barely above a whisper. He knew the teller in the next booth was focused on her customer's transaction.

"Call you later," Julia responded. "Thank you."

With that she left the bank, being careful to walk in her pony gait, just in case he was stealing a glance at her rear end.

Julia called James at seven that evening, and they set up a dinner date for the following evening at six. He promised to take her to a "nice little place" he knew. She did not ask for details. She didn't much care. Julia thought she needed at least one romantic interest while in Paris, even though becoming involved in a serious relationship was the farthest thing from her mind. She was just going to live from day to day, enjoy herself as much as she could, and see how long it took her to become bored with that city. Something told her that would eventually be the case. Then, she would be out of there, back to the States, and on her way to San

Francisco. Unlike the case with her stay in Paris, Julia did have plans for San Francisco, California. She was sure she could make a decent life for herself there. Wasn't that the same city in which one of these older singers had left his heart? The melody of the song was starting in her head, and she went right into humming it. She regretted not knowing the words of any but the first line of the song. She had heard her mother singing it on a couple of occasions, but hadn't paid close attention. It was the music of an older generation.

Chapter 8

At home, Cora curled up on the couch, cradled the cordless phone between her neck and left shoulder, and listened to Charlotte's account of Mike's most recent troubles. Lately, Mike's life had been so dark, Charlotte reported in a low, sorrowful tone. Rain was streaming down Cora's window panes, and she knew that if it were raining where Mike was now, his mood would be even darker still. As far as Charlotte knew, Mike was close to a nervous breakdown over the allegations of threatened murder and arson. He declared his innocence to anyone who would listen, but he couldn't get his alibis together, and Satan's experiencing a cold day in hell was more likely to happen than his being able to clear his name. His closest friends were already giving him the cold shoulder, not wanting to express an opinion one way or the other, and his wife mostly gave him the silent treatment simply because she didn't know what to think or what to say to him. Mike had also taken an unpaid leave of absence from work because he couldn't function efficiently under all the stress and had trouble just getting out of bed in the morning. When she last called his house, she had been told by his wife that he never left his room except to use the bathroom, and was refusing to get help for his depression. His wife, Charlotte reported to Cora, was not taking kindly to the sudden shortage of money or his present physical condition, and was trying to decide what to do with herself. She had no plans on living like this 'til the whole mess cleared. Thank God they had no children. Divorce would be easy. He could keep the house. She had met him with it, and their other assets had remained separate.

In Cora's mind, events were unfolding for Mike just as she had hoped they would. It was all she could do to keep from interjecting words like 'great' or 'serves-him-right' as each bit of news fell on her eager ears. She wished that his saga of misery would go on for a long, long time, and he would live the rest of his life as a sad and bitter old man. In fact, she hoped he would wind up doing a stint in prison, and having the added sting of knowing he was doing time for a crime he didn't commit burned into his brain for the rest of his life, overshadowing everything pleasant that he had ever known. Cora knew that she didn't want him dead. She wanted him alive and wishing he were dead. She wanted him deeply unhappy and immeasurably miserable.

Chapter 9

James picked Julia up promptly at six. In his jeans, loafers, and crisp white shirt with an open collar, he looked even sexier than he had when she first saw him at the bank. She would be happy to be seen with him in public.

"Hi, Julia." James said, grinning at Julia.

"Gee, you drive my car!"

"What do you mean?"

"I own the same car back in the States."

"Oh, yeah? What color?"

"The same color."

"That's cute. Ready to eat?"

"Sure thing."

The two headed for the "nice little place" that James had mentioned earlier. It turned out to be a small restaurant with an intimate ambience, dimly lit; a pianist doing a jazz number just beyond the entrance and to the left. They requested a table in the non-smoking section, and were seated right away. The waiter arrived and rattled off the specials, but Julia didn't listen, and asked James to order for her. She knew that on a date she should order her food first and the gentleman should order after her, that was the protocol, but she didn't feel like doing it that way. She had learned that from Clayton. It was also the way he and Cora did things. Julia didn't think she needed to be that formal. She'd have a Pellegrino with a twist of lemon, no appetizer. The rest was up to him. She wasn't a picky eater. The grilled mushrooms stuffed with crabmeat that James ordered for both of them was a little overdone, but other than that, dinner went well. James ordered Crème Bruleè afterward. Julia declined her own desert and had a taste of his; just enough to kill the residual taste of the entrée. Besides, she was an American. Americans were either perpetually watchful of their waistline, or didn't give a heck about it; nothing in-between.

Their dinner conversation had been pleasant and easy, and Julia thought James seemed to be the safe, well-balanced, and wholesome type. He played tennis or golf for relaxation; she couldn't really remember which one he'd said all of those two minutes ago. She was not into sports at all. Attending Charlie's hockey games back in the States had been just for the sake of supporting Charlie. Julia pursed her lips as she thought to herself that she couldn't believe Charlie was dead, dead as a doornail. She realized that she had remembered the words, *Morley was dead, dead as a doornail* from a book written by Charles Dickens. She didn't remember which book it was. They had made her read all this literature in high school. What a waste!

Reaching her flat at the end of the date, Julia invited James in, and the two got into deep kissing and heavy petting, but she would eventually refuse his further sexual advances, and he would force himself on her. This time, however, she did not cry, or hide herself in shame and pain the way she had when Charlie raped her. Instead, she was brave and tearless, and after it was all over, she threatened to report James to the police, as well as his bank manager, except he could make it up to her in some way.

She still had the envelope with his name and number and request to call him in her possession. Sure she had agreed to a date, but certainly not to rape, she would say to anyone who dared query her role in this. James, realizing what he'd done and knowing that it was never his original intention to take the girl by force, was wracked with guilt and shame, and begged her to forgive him. Truthfully, he told her that he was much more concerned about not being forgiven by her, than he was about being reported to the police or his boss. Julia let him know that her forgiveness would come with a price. She ordered him to take another look at the previous day's transactions, re-access Clayton's funds, and transfer additional sums of money into her account. He was to transfer small amounts, say four or five hundred dollars at a time, over the next several weeks starting the next day. She would let him know when she wanted him to stop. Julia remembered Clayton mentioning that the funds he was sending her would come out of a six-month certificate of deposit that he had no intention of cashing in. It was money that he just kept rolling over every time the maturity date came around. He didn't even really keep tabs on the account to see how much it made. He had instructed his banker to continue doing automatic rollovers until further notice. The funds had just matured, coincidentally, so he would call his banker and have the transfer done before starting the new term. Julia didn't know how much money Clayton was talking about or what kind of time frame he was working within, as far as maturity of the certificate and the beginning of the new term. She just figured that with Clayton's status in his company and the money he must make, it had to be a hefty sum, and that Clayton would wait at least a couple of weeks between sending her the money and calling his banker again. He would not incur any penalties for pre-mature or interim withdrawals, and if he did, so what? She would work fast.

James said that he would do it. He would do anything, as long as she was willing to forgive him. Once he agreed to this pilfering of funds from Clayton's account and uncharacteristically dishonest behavior, James felt the crème brulee he'd had for desert beginning to repeat on him. He pecked Julia on the cheek, and instead of saying goodnight said: "I'm so sorry."

Julia let James out without saying anything further, and stood with her left hand on the handle of the closed door for several minutes, trying to grasp the weight of the predicament she had just put him in. However, she soon brushed the thought aside and reasoned that both James and Clayton needed to pay for their stupidity, as well as for Charlie's sins. Julia had always thought Clayton was dumb, virtually kissing her mother's feet to marry her, and being rejected time and time again. Now, this other clown had gotten himself in hot water because he couldn't keep his fly zipped. Well, whatever! Besides, she was the one who had been violated. Twice. Charlie had gotten away with it (the suicide had been his own decision). This James person needed to pay. It suddenly occurred to Julia that if Charlie hadn't already killed himself, she could find a way to get money out of him for raping her. She was sorry she hadn't thought of that before. Too late now. This deal with James was not something she had planned. It was just a bright idea that had come to her out of nowhere. Clayton was paying in cold cash; no problem there.

"Well," Julia thought, "What one loses on the swing, one can gain on the roundabout. It's all part of life's little games."

James spent most of that night rolling around in his bed, wondering how he could get out of the mess he'd gotten himself into in one moment of indiscretion. Prior to this evening, neither theft nor fraud had ever entered his mind, and the idea of doing it on someone else's behalf seemed even more far fetched. He didn't think that he could go ahead with Julia's proposal, but at the time, he couldn't think of a response other than one that was agreeable. He was no good at thinking on his feet. What he did know, was that he needed to come up with an escape route, an alternate plan. By the time sleep got the better of him, he had decided that he would just go to work the following day and hope that Julia had had a change of heart. If she hadn't, he had no idea what he would do.

By nine thirty the next morning, James, who had begun the day on a relatively calm note considering what had happened the night before, suddenly began to experience a serious case of the jitters. Julia had walked into the bank, added her name to the list of people waiting to see an administrator, and took a seat in the little waiting area at the front of the bank. James had no idea why she was there. Had she decided to report him for something? Would she report him for asking her to call? Was she going to report the rape? She had not even given him a chance to get those transactions moving. Why was she there? It was only nine thirty, for God's sake! Or was she there on other business? James tried to keep his mind focused on the business at hand. The customer at his window was cashing a check and wanted her account balance. The line waiting in between the ropes was quite long, and growing longer. The bank seemed always crowded at this time of day. Things would taper off between ten and eleven, and start getting busy again between eleven thirty and one o'clock. He wished that Julia had come in during the slow hours. He stole glances at her as he tried to conduct business with his customers. Her nose was buried in a magazine, and she seemed focused on what she was reading. She did not look up. He was sure she would hear her name when her turn came and she was called into one of the cubicles, but for now she seemed oblivious to everything and everyone around her.

Julia's presence at the bank made James very nervous, and he noticed that his palms were hot and sweaty as he tried to control his shaking hands while counting out his customer's money. As soon as the customer left the window, James put up the 'closed' sign and went to the men's room. When he returned four or five minutes later, Julia was nowhere to be found. He scanned the waiting room. He scanned the cubicles. He looked through the big glass doors. Maybe she had just come in for cash and had decided to use the ATM outside the main door of the bank. He scanned that line. No Julia.

Julia had left the bank. She had correctly calculated that her presence there first thing in the morning would unnerve James. She had actually gone in just to remind him that he had her business to take care of as discussed the night before, but had no intention of speaking to him. Just seeing her would be enough of a reminder—and a threat. She would sit for a while, and then slip away. What she was going to do was check her account balance by phone at the end of the business day, and if the account didn't show a transfer of funds into it, she would call James at home and casually ask for his boss's name and direct line. That move should guarantee quick action on his part. Julia sat around her apartment the rest of the day doing nothing in particular, checked her account at around 7:00 P.M. and put in a phone call to James. He calmly gave her the information she requested, pretending that he was not the least bit worried about why she wanted it.

Another sleepless night, however, brought him to his senses. James decided that he had to become proactive about the situation he now found himself in. He would go in tomorrow and talk to his boss about Julia's proposal. He would come clean about being immediately attracted to her, and slipping her his phone number before he had time to really think about what he was doing. He also would ask if there were rules that forbade employees to do that sort of thing. He really didn't know. He would explain about the date, and his sexual exploit. It hadn't actually been rape. They were kind of halfway there already with all the deep kissing and mutual heavy petting. He was sure his boss, being a man himself, would understand the situation from a male perspective. Attractive women were hard to resist. He would let his boss know that if he needed to aid an investigation by continuing to date Julia while wearing a wire, he would do so. Obviously, this gorgeous woman had no moral compass, and cared only about herself. He was not going to let her ruin his career. He was twenty-five years old, and knew he could have a long and successful future ahead of him if he didn't blow it. He wasn't going to.

Chapter 10

Thelma, these last days, was finding that with Gilbert gone she was a little more relaxed, not quite as angry, and more inclined to engage in conversation with the other members of her small crew. She still had the Ken and Cora issue unresolved, but generally speaking, she was relaxed and a lot more open than she had been. Maybe openness could be beneficial to her in the end, she reasoned. For starters, one of her conversations with Ken had sort of led her to her daughter, Cora. She didn't know where she was, not yet, but she was sure she would find that out by and by. She hadn't immediately started blurting out questions the minute Ken's story registered with her. That would not have been prudent; and Thelma was nothing, if not prudent. Her life so far had demanded that of her. She was sure that at some future time she'd be able to revisit that story with Ken and find out more. He and Cora were out of touch, but maybe he still knew her whereabouts, or knew someone who knew. She still had to decide whether or not she wanted to reconnect with her daughter. She had to decide whether she wanted Ken dead or alive. She was thinking that she should not take Ken's life just yet, anyway. If she killed him before she'd gotten all the information that she wanted about Cora, it would not be exactly pointless, but it would be the waste of a golden opportunity to do whatever it was she was going to do, or find out about her daughter.

Thelma thought she'd seek out Clarence. She wondered if his silence and reserve, so similar to hers, was covering up something; some sinister past, some tragic story like her own. She knew that her own secrets and troubles could make Pandora's Box seem like child's play. Thelma figured that if the seemingly open, carefree, and outgoing Ken had secrets in his past, then the silent, pensive, emotionally distant Clarence must have even more.

Chapter 11

Day dawned with a cloudless sky; the temperature was gradually warming. It was a beautiful day, and Clarence decided to spend it on deck, alone, communing with nature. He was seeking the "oceanic feeling" that the philosopher Jean-Jacques Rousseau experienced after a horse had kicked him unconscious. Clarence wanted his being to be fused with everything around him. He wanted to feel the oneness between himself and the universe at large. That was for him a kind of meditation. He was unaware of Thelma's approach or arrival on the deck until she spoke.

"Hi Ya!" The woman greeted Clarence.

"Hi."

"Nice day."

"Yep."

"What are you thinking about?"

"Nothing."

"Would you ever murder anyone?"

"Nope."

"Why not?"

"Because everything and everyone is here for a reason, and will leave the earth in their own time."

"How about someone who really hurt you and ruined your life?"

"No one can ruin your life without ruining their own, so revenge is kind of redundant."

"I don't get it."

"Your getting it, or not getting it does not affect the truth of it—fortunately."

"I don't agree."

"Okay."

"I'd like to explore that idea. I totally do not agree."

"Well, maybe some other time. I really just want to enjoy the day. It's just so glorious."

With that, Thelma turned and left, muttering to herself that Clarence was even weirder than she first imagined him to be. She didn't get it. She might as well forget it. She meant to converse with him a bit about his perspective on life, and possibly get some advice, but it was almost impossible to talk to him. She would have to come to her own conclusions about things. To kill or not to kill, that was her question. She could tell that it was going to be a very lonely decision-making process.

Chapter 12

The bank manager regretted having to tell James that the police would not arrest Julia just because some bank manager and his employee said that she was considering getting one of them to commit acts of fraud. That just wasn't the way things were done. Europe was a different kind of continent. The police didn't even tote guns around. James would have to show proof of being coerced into committing a crime, and actually commit a crime. Right now, it would be just his word against hers. As for James's giving Julia his phone number, that was no big deal, and what happened between employees and their friends after work hours was not the bank's concern. With regard to the proposed fraud issue, they would just have to wait for Julia's next move.

James left his boss's office resolving to entrap the girl and clear himself from this web of trouble. He would invite her out again, bring up the difficulty he was having moving the money, and record their conversation.

Once again, Julia checked her bank balance and realized that still, no additional monies had been transferred into her account. In a split second, her mind softened and she decided that having given James something to worry about was probably enough punishment. After all, she hadn't exactly hated the sexual experience. It had been a lot less forceful than the experience with Charlie, and not half as painful, physically, since she was no longer a virgin. Besides, she had thought that she could trust Charlie, and expected his respect. She had no expectations of James. He didn't know her. Julia figured that she was judging her most recent sexual experience this way partly because it was no longer her first time, and partly because she had herself been aroused to some degree, having willingly participated in the foreplay. Whatever the reason, she would just let the money issue slide; at least for now. She would let the guy continue his career in peace. Sure she'd date him again. She would simply wipe that whole afternoon out of her memory for good; wouldn't even mention the original proposal.

Before James could put part two of his plan into action and ask Julia out on another date, she left for California. She didn't contact him to talk about the plan anymore, or to say that she was leaving. Failing to reach Julia by phone over a two-day period, James stopped by her flat after work and was told by the landlady that Julia had left for California the day before. The landlady didn't know when, or if, Julia was coming back. She lived there on a week-to-week basis and no rent was outstanding. She hadn't given any prior notice about leaving. She had just knocked on the door, suitcases in hand, said she was leaving and turned in the key to the flat. The landlady had not bothered to ask any questions.

"Young people are a strange lot," she said, partly to herself, partly to James. "I've never had children of my own but I've heard enough stories about the weird behavior of my teenage nieces and nephews from my siblings. There is no telling what is going on in their minds from one moment to the other. This Julia seems to be another directionless one. I wonder if her parents even know where she is."

James thanked the woman and returned to his apartment. He didn't know what to think, but with no Julia to date, and no way to prove his story to his boss, there was nothing more to do about that matter for now.

Chapter 13

Back in the USA, and in California, as she had so many times envisioned herself being, Julia felt like her old self again, but with an added quality. She no longer felt like the fragile girl that had left school prematurely and headed out to Paris without a plan. She felt gorgeous, which indeed she was, and womanly. She was also inwardly amused by the fact that she was once again in the same state and country as Cora, and that her mother had no idea she was there. She wondered how many degrees of separation existed between them. Maybe six; just like the movie. Maybe twelve, given the way things were between them now. Julia laughed out loud and thought that she had probably inherited her mother's quirky sense of humor. She knew she shouldn't be laughing, but she was.

San Francisco was just as beautiful as ever, and very much the way she had been picturing it in her mind forever now. Her first order of business, she knew, was to find a small hotel that would give her a good price for a month's stay, but she couldn't resist the temptation to have the cab driver drop her off in the middle of Union Square so she could get a look in the stores, luggage and all, before looking for a place to stay. In fact, she thought that a salesperson in one of the stores might have a valuable lead as to where she could reside. She was right. A woman at the BCBG Max Azria outlet directed her to Bush Avenue where there were several reasonable hotels. It was a short walk from the store, according to the woman, but because Julia was beginning to feel a little tired from the weight of her luggage, she stepped onto the sidewalk and flagged down a cab to take her there. A big sign that read La Maison caught Julia's eye, and she asked the driver to drop her off there. She hoped they at least had room for one for tonight. If she liked it, she would talk to the concierge about monthly arrangements tomorrow. If not, she could move out the next day. Right now, she needed to put her stuff down and stretch out somewhere. She was in luck. There was one room left on the third floor— a room overlooking the street. Clients refused it because they wanted to avoid the street noise and the sound of busy traffic. Julia took the elevator up to her room, threw herself across the bed and fell into a deep sleep. When she woke up, she saw that the little digital clock on her nightstand read 5:30 A.M.

She felt rested enough to grab a shower then, and change into some fresh clothing. When things came to life around there, she would check out the hotel's amenities and decide whether to stay or ask for more references. Julia actually thought it might be more economical to stay at some kind of motor inn; a Motel 6 or was it 9? She wasn't sure she could find one in that city. It wasn't Vegas that catered to the cultured and the coarse alike. She'd have to see. This place was kind of cozy, and centrally located. That was important since she didn't yet have a vehicle. From here she could walk to the stores and find most of what she wanted. Public transportation was also easily available. That was a plus.

La Maison turned out to be adequate enough for Julia's purposes right now. She decided that she'd better begin job hunting, and then look for another place when she found employment. That way, she'd know exactly how much money she'd have at her disposal for rent and other living expenses. San Francisco was an expensive city to live in, she'd heard. That plan made more sense. She still had a chunk of Clayton's money so she'd be fine for a while if she could keep her clothes shopping down to a minimum.

Julia knew that level of restraint would be a challenge for her. Later that day, she talked to the concierge about a monthly rate. The older gentleman thought he'd enjoy seeing her around the place, since he found her to be exceptionally beautiful, and made her an offer that she found irresistible.

Finding a job did not turn out to be hard for Julia either. She went out later that day and approached the finer hotels first, as she had planned to do since she began mapping out her California life back in Paris, and they were eager to hire her. They were not, however, offering her nearly enough money, she thought. How was a girl supposed to shop and keep herself looking good? How did they expect her to live on such a small salary? Besides, these were front desk positions welcoming and registering guests; there were no tips to be had, Julia thought, slightly annoyed. Did they think that all she needed to do was pay for transportation to and from work? She figured that most girls her age probably still lived at home, and could make do on a pittance, but she could not.

On her way home to La Maison that evening Julia spotted a sign that read "Welcome to China Town," and made the right turn that took her down Grant Street and right into the heart of it. The narrow street was lined on both sides with a gazillion stores selling pretty much the same ware: tee shirts, magnets, key chains, purses, little pyramid looking things; Julia couldn't think of the name for them. Some vendors had set up trays on the sidewalk in front of their stores to more easily advertise their goods. A few restaurants were dotted in between the stores. There was a lot to see, but nothing she really wanted to buy except for a little toad made of green Murano glass that she saw in one of the windows. She went in to price it. The cost was ten dollars, the storekeeper said. It was cute, and Julia smiled as she reflected on her romantic life. So far it had consisted of kissing three toads, one against her will, one against *his* will, sort of, and one with mutual consent. Julia smiled to herself and shuddered at the same time. She would get the little toad for her nightstand. The salesman carefully put the ornament in bubble wrap, taped it all around, and handed it to Julia. She stuffed it into her pocketbook, handed him seven dollars, and walked toward the door. As she stepped onto the pavement, she heard the salesman yelling: "Miss!" realizing that she had given him three dollars short of the price he'd asked, but Julia didn't turn around. She now stepped into the middle of the street, made her way between two cars and crossed to the other side, continuing in the direction that she was initially headed.

Her mind had already gone back to her quest for work. Julia thought she would have to consider dancing at a strip joint if the salaries she'd been offered so far were par for the course in 'decent' places. There was just no way a girl could live well on such measly salaries, and she sure as hell was not doing two jobs, or working seven days a week. She also needed to have her weekends free for hanging out in Sausalito. It was all part of her dream for life in California: her freedom, the encounters with celebrity, or at least a glimpse at them, the obsession with physical appearance, the shopping.

With that decision made, Julia began on what was now day 3, looking for work as an exotic dancer. She had no experience at dancing or stripping, but imagined that it couldn't be that hard to swing oneself around a pole half naked, and strike seductive poses halfway up or down one. She would practice leg raises and deep squats at home, and figure out what to do with her eyes when she stooped down to look into the eyes of one of her grinning middle-aged male customers. She'd be able to move to the music, she was sure. That whole thing about black people being born dancers and having natural rhythm had better kick in now. She stopped in the middle of the sidewalk, took two little salsa steps forward, and two backward. "Not salsa moves!" Julia admonished herself, "Erotic moves." She continued down the street in her normal gait. She would have to tell her prospective employers that she had had jobs as an exotic dancer when she lived in Paris. They were hardly likely to call overseas to check.

As Julia strolled along the sidewalks, she noticed that *The Kinky Kitten* had just the outfits that she would need for her night performances if she did indeed get a job as a dancer. The shop's display windows showed lots of stringy little numbers that covered just the crotch and nipples. For now, Julia figured she'd buy something in black and something in red. Maybe she should wait, but what the heck! She was sure she wanted to do this. These colors went best with her light complexion and voluminous tresses of jet-black hair. If things went well, she would expand her wardrobe. After a week or so, maybe she could talk the club's owners into paying for her getups. She'd have to wait and see.

First find the job. She had a bright idea. Why not wear one of the little getups to the interview. She would layer it under her trench coat. A trench coat in San Francisco was commonplace. It was always a little cool there, especially in the morning. She decided that after the introduction of herself and handshake with the prospective employer, she would undo the buttons and sit with the coat wide open. Her arms would remain in the sleeves, but she would slide the neckline off her shoulders to reveal her

Double-D cups to the full gaze of the employer. That would be a pretty sight——and irresistible. A surefire strategy for getting hired.

That night Julia went to bed in a great frame of mind. The mere thought of working at a strip club had her tingling all over with excitement. She had now looked around and made a list of the places she would target first. She envisioned men licking their lips as she shook her breasts so close to their faces she could feel their breath on her bosom. She knew they were not allowed to touch her. She could immediately call security and have them thrown out of the facility. She pictured large fingers reaching up to stuff hundred-dollar bills in her garters, still without touching her. True, the people she'd meet at the club would most likely be a bunch of perverts, but who cared? She knew the rules of these clubs though she couldn't recall how she had learned of them. She knew that she could dance with and talk to patrons, but not date them. The patrons knew the rules, too, so she was safe. At least these people had money to burn, and she was more than happy to take some of it. She wasn't stealing. They were paying to play.

Julia smiled comfortably in her belief that people did not go to hell when they died, if they were bad while living on earth. She felt that every soul would be given one last chance, just before the very end, to set things right. She was sure she would have a moment to repent. Right now, it was about doing what she needed to do to make life on earth doable. God was, after all, an understanding god, and one who wanted the best for all his children. If he hadn't struck her down at the mere thought of stripping in the presence of strange men, then it must be okay with him. Julia laughed again, and thought that she liked her own sense of humor better than anyone else's. She hoped that the good Lord had a sense of humor as well. Besides, why would death even knock on her door? She was still only a teenager; not close to having used up her allotted three score and ten years.

Chapter 14

Cora's heart was happy hearing reports of Mike's suffering, and she really felt that the S-O-B had not suffered nearly enough to quell *her* pain. If only she could find a way to let him know that his darling wife was beginning to transfer her affections to another man. Since Mike's arrest and subsequent depression, nothing had been happening in the marital bed, so Cora had been told. She knew that Mike's penis had a mind of its own even in good times, and he had said so himself. Imagine now that he was under severe stress. **OMG!** It would not be quite a surprise if "wifey" decided to seek sexual satisfaction elsewhere. Cora thought she could have someone call and act as though he were the other man. He could call during the day when Mike was home alone, and ask for the woman of the house; refuse to leave a message or say who he was, and somehow let Mike know that he was sleeping with his wife. The problem was that Cora didn't have any male friends she could put up to the prank. Clayton would never stoop to something so low and he would be appalled and disgusted if he knew what she was up to. There had to be something else she could do to take Mike's life farther down the road to a living hell. She was not nearly, oh not nearly, done with him.

As she sat at her kitchen table trying to formulate part two of her plan for Mike's destruction, the phone rang. It startled Cora almost out of her skin, and she immediately snatched it out of its cradle to stop it from ringing. It was Clayton. His voice was deep and silky. She hadn't heard it in a while. She suddenly realized that she missed him. She remembered now how he sounded when he talked to her, as they sat together on the couch so many times in the past; he with his back up against one of the arms, legs outstretched on the seat cushions, she sitting in the inverted V formed by his legs, with her back up against his torso and his arms around her middle. His voice brought his handsome features to her mind presently.

"Julia?" Clayton said into his receiver.

"Julia's mother."

"Gee! Cora! It's Clayton. How are you?"

"Good. How are **you**?"

"Good. I'm doing real well. How are you?"

"You asked me that. How was your trip? It's been a while."

"Trip was good. Quite good. Anything new?"

"Not on this side, no."

"Yeah, the trip was good. Good trip."

Clayton was obviously fumbling in his effort to make what should have been easy conversation with her, and Cora knew with certainty that something was up, but she had no idea what that was. This was a retarded kind of exchange going on between them; very unlike the conversations she was used to having with her man. Clayton was obviously hiding something, guilty of something, or nervous about something. She wondered if he was getting ready to pose that marriage question again, but she quickly dismissed that idea because he had just gone off on a trip without her, and she was sure he had been back in town for several days,

169

and was only now calling. He had also just called her Julia, but maybe she sounded like her daughter and Clayton thought that Julia had come back from Paris. That was not so strange, perhaps.

"Are you stopping by?"

"No. I just wanted to say hello. Haven't spoken to you."

"Well, hello. Speak to me."

"Well there's nothing. I thought I'd get around to visiting Julia for a minute while I was in Paris, but things got very hectic and I didn't get to see her. My time there just went by really fast. Well, you know Paris! There's always so much to take up your time. You think you're going to do a few specific things and the next thing you know you're doing forty other things and then you're back on the plane coming back home. It's really amazing how that happens. Paris is an amazing place, just truly amazing."

Clayton had gone from bumbling and repeating himself to talking in a blue streak, and Cora remained perfectly silent while he rattled off all those sentences and explanations. She tried to listen for something in his tone, something in his choice of words, something in his breathing, something that would give away his secret, because she was now sure that he had one.

"Oh, I'm sure Julia's fine." Cora managed to interject. "I spoke with her the other day."

"Good."

"Yeah."

"Well, let me run. I'm just in from the office. I'll be in touch."

Before Cora could say goodbye, she heard the click of the receiver on the other end. There was definitely something to his not inviting her to go with him on that last trip to France. He was probably depressed about her latest refusal to marry him. He was probably seeing someone else. Maybe he found out that she'd been out of town and was wondering if she was having a relationship that he didn't know about. Cora decided that there were too many questions she couldn't answer without his help. She would get in her car and drive over to his place. They might as well talk about whatever the problem was. Then again, maybe there was no problem. It could be that she was letting that imagination of hers run away; down the streets of infidelity and betrayal, jealousy and suspicion. Those questions she had just asked herself were all very silly. What could be wrong? This was Clayton. He had been hers for some time now. She would just drive over there. It would be nice to see him and talk face to face. Without changing clothes she grabbed her purse and keys, got into her car and headed toward Clayton's house. He had just called her from home; he should still be there.

Cora drove the route she had taken several times before without noticing any of the scenery. She left home, and she arrived at her destination seemingly suddenly. As she began the left turn into Clayton's driveway, she saw his green Land Rover backing out. Cora stopped, put her car in reverse and backed up several yards so he could get out without obstruction. She now put her foot on the brake, and shifted the gear stick back to the Drive position. As Clayton's window lined up with the window on her passenger side, Cora noticed that her man wasn't alone. A dark-haired Caucasian woman, who at a glance appeared to be in her late thirties, was in the passenger seat. She turned and looked expressionlessly at Cora. Cora knew she had never seen the woman before. She leaned just slightly towards Clayton's window, touched her horn lightly, and got his attention.

"Were you coming to see me?" Clayton asked pleasantly.

"Yes." Cora said, trying to smile while swallowing a lump in her throat.

"Let me call you when I get back."

With that Clayton finished backing out, gave a short sharp slightly right turn to his steering wheel, then straightened the car and started driving off in the opposite direction from which Cora had come.

Cora pulled her head back without responding, and kept her foot on the brake until Clayton's vehicle was completely out of the way. She was momentarily rendered speechless, breathless, emotionless, and numb. Her mind seemed to contain no thoughts. She watched him leave without saying anything more to her than that he would call her when he got back. She straightened up her car from its slightly left-bent position, and stepped gently on the gas. For the first hundred yards or so, she followed behind the two in the green Land Rover. She realized that she could not see into the vehicle because of the tinted windows. Now the Land Rover turned left. Cora kept straight on. She decided to take the long way back home. She had to let her mind replay what had just happened and try to figure it all out.

Thirty-five minutes later, Cora burst into her front door, threw herself on the sofa and pulled out her cell phone to dial Julia's number. She put the phone down on the coffee table. That would be a million dollars; calling overseas from her cell phone at this time of day. She had gotten herself one of those prepaid numbers with anytime minutes, but the minutes were quite expensive. It wasn't because she couldn't afford a phone with super features and a great calling plan, but she thought it was unnecessary. She really just needed to make a call and take a call—and that, only once in a blue moon, such as when she was en route to a meeting or something, and needed to say she was running late, or almost there, or maybe she'd have to clarify the directions to her destination. Cora had a way of driving most of her route without a hitch, and then getting lost just when she had to make those final turns onto side roads and find the street she was supposed to be on. She had considered purchasing a GPS, and decided against it.

She now walked into the kitchen to use her land line. She picked up the receiver, and then thought she'd better call from her bedroom where she would have more privacy. Although Cora was alone in her house, she somehow felt that her bedroom would afford her more privacy than the kitchen would. She put the receiver back in its cradle and went up to her room. Once there, she sat on the chaise lounge, took the phone off the nightstand, placed it on her lap and dialed Julia's number. She let the phone ring fifteen times, or twenty, she wasn't sure. There was no answer.

Unable to reach her daughter, Cora felt emotion rush through her like waves of a tsunami. The thought of having been with yet another man and losing him drove her almost insane. She buried her face in her hands and cried from way deep inside herself. Every cell in her body seemed tremulous and wracked with pain. It wasn't one big pain that affected every cell. She felt that each cell was experiencing its own pain and registering it in her soul. How long she wept and rocked herself in agony, she didn't know, but her head was throbbing wildly now, and she felt a cold sweat forming on her brow. It wasn't even about losing Clayton, really. It was about having another relationship go down the tubes. Was she ever going to have someone whom she cherished and who cherished her forever? She finally got a grip on herself and decided that she would not jump to conclusions, at the same time wondering if she was slipping into denial. Which was it? Cora didn't know for sure.

She walked into the bathroom and put cold water on her face. She felt calmer. She would wait until she could talk to Clayton and find out exactly what was going on with their relationship. She was sure he'd be home before too long. It couldn't be over between them. Nothing had really happened. Their last conversation had been a little strange, but they hadn't had a quarrel, and there was no other hint of a problem. He had probably just had a very long day. That could have been a co-worker in his car. He could have been giving her a ride home from the office, but had swung by his place first for some reason; maybe just to hear her voice; but then he carried a cell phone. He could have used that.

Oh, really. I don't know what to think. I would really just have to wait and talk.

Deep inside her mind, however, Cora knew there was some correlation—maybe several correlations—between refusing to marry Clayton, his trip to France without her, his waiting several days before calling her when he was back in town, his calling her by her daughter's name, the weird nature of their most recent conversation, and the strange woman in his SUV, but she didn't know which two or three things to put together. She had to talk to him.

Chapter 15

Julia's first two nights as a dancer at *Babes* went extremely well. It seemed to her employers that she was very experienced, and she, Julia, dubbed herself a natural. The club owners had told her during her break on the very first night that she could work as many nights as she wanted. They thought she was great, and she was a fresh, new face at the club. Patrons liked that. Julia told them that she would think about it and let them know. She knew she didn't want to work on Fridays, Saturdays, or Sundays, but would be willing to cover for a girl here and there, if someone really had to have a weekend off.

As fate would have it, Jolie, a girl Julia had chatted casually with at the club when she worked on that first night, had a death in her family, and someone was needed to work in her place. It was on that very first weekend of Julia's stint at the place. The owners immediately approached her, and although she was unwilling to deviate from her decisions about her work schedule so early in the game, she considered the fact that she was new on the job, and thought she'd better show herself as being a team player, and willing employee. She knew she'd have nothing to lose and everything to gain if management perceived her as being dedicated and easy to work with. Julia agreed to cover for Jolie, and by the end of the Saturday night gig, had figured out that the bulk of a dancer's money was made on weekends; middle-aged men having stuffed fifty-dollar bills into her garters and shoes, and the crook of her elbow when she stooped down hugging the dance pole and swaying her rear end. Julia's eyes accidentally caught a glimpse of the clock on the back wall of the salon. Along with the club music, another sound started running through her mind. It was the voice that she had often heard on TV saying, "It's 10 p.m. Do you know where your children are?" She wondered if Cora was trying to answer that question now. She thought there had to be wives at home trying to answer the question, too: "It's now 10 p.m. Do you know where your husband is?" She half smiled and licked her lips as she lined her face up with a patron's. He seemed to be about 60. He licked his lips, too, and grinned at the guy next to him.

In two nights, Julia had taken in four times what she had made all of that week doing the weeknight stint. She went to her employers to talk about changing her schedule. She'd rather work Thursday through Sunday, and have three nights off together at the beginning of the week, if it was okay with them. Hanging out in Sausalito could wait a minute, she was thinking now.

Management had no objections to her proposal. In fact, they were eager to oblige, and moved around the schedules of a few girls (without consulting them) in order to accommodate Julia with the new arrangements she wanted. They could see without looking too hard that this new gem of a girl could bring a lot of money into the establishment. As far as they were concerned, everybody would win, and that made their decision to agree to the new arrangements a no-brainer.

Chapter 16

So while Julia danced and Cora vacillated between her feelings of bewilderment about the situation with Clayton and her burning desire to settle the score with Mike, Clayton cemented his relationship with Amy, who was the new woman in his life. She had been in his life for several years as a friend and co-worker, and knew of Cora's existence, sort of vaguely. Clayton had noticed that of all his co-workers, Amy was the one he could count on for an honest opinion about his position and handling of things. Sometimes she was honest enough to hurt his feelings, if he allowed himself to take it the wrong way. She was, however, always respectful and Clayton felt that, around her, it was safe to be flawed. She never seemed to worry about having to protect the friendship between them. In the last several weeks, though, things had escalated between them. They seemed to recognize a surge in their feelings for each other at the same time and spoke about it. Clayton, being the gentleman that he was, told Amy that he would like to establish a serious relationship with her after he had completely broken off his relationship with Cora. Amy knew that she could wait. They would, however, begin some casual dating. It would give her time to endear herself to him, and Clayton would not be made to feel that he was cheating. She also appreciated the fact that he was not the kind of man who wanted to see two women at the same time. It was a noble stance, considering the way men generally were these days. They rarely left a relationship until a new one was securely in place, or they were sure to start a new relationship the minute they felt the old one beginning to slip away. It was nice that Clayton wanted to end one relationship, before seriously pursuing another. That spoke volumes about the kind of husband he would be.

Clayton knew he could wait, too. He needed time to decide when and how Cora would be informed that it was over between them, and that he would be moving on. He was also thinking that maybe Cora would figure it out and leave without his having to ask her to. He didn't know which scenario would play out first. It was not that he was trying to eat his cake and have it. He wasn't that type. He just wanted to do this thing in the way that was least difficult for everyone involved, and still end up getting what he wanted now, which was out of that old relationship with Cora, and fully into this new one with Amy. He had been listening to his Tony Robins tapes, and had decided that a fully functional romantic relationship, with the outcome of marriage and children was the thing he was after now. He had also just bought a new house and thought it would be nice to share it with a woman. He had spoken to Cora about that, too, and the idea had been rejected. It wasn't happening with her, and he was really ready to move on.

Several weeks later, he would listen in amazement as he heard himself, as though he were outside of his own body, telling Cora in a most impassioned tone that having a family was what life was all about. That's exactly what he wanted. He knew that she was not going that route. So there it was! If she didn't get from that conversation that he was out of her life now, she would never get it. He made sure to repeat the point a few times just to be sure she knew what he was saying. His plan, although spontaneously hatched, worked like a charm. When Cora and he began that conversation, Clayton had no idea where it was going, or what they were going to be talking about. It did not start out being a conversation about their relationship, per se. It was just another one of his phone calls to her. Of course, he knew the opportunity would arise at some point, to tell her how he felt, but he didn't know when, or how, and he wasn't forcing the issue. He knew it would come to him, which ironically, was something Cora always told him when he was trying to decide what to do or say about something. Sometime earlier, Clayton had mentioned to Cora having gotten the tapes. She had listened without a show of much interest. He mentioned some ideas he had picked up from them. She'd said that they were good. She was thinking that they had listened to motivational tapes like those before and neither one of them had followed through for long enough to make a difference in their lives. Usually after a few weeks, they would slide back into their old modus operandi. What was so different now? But then came the talk of passionate relationships and family. What he hadn't mentioned, was that he was working through the tapes with Amy, and they were making a decision to operate their lives in that way together. They had both been looking for something more fulfilling than they'd had in their past and current relationships. It was the right time for Amy; it was also the right time for Clayton. Their desires were in concert, and they could feel the mingling of their spirits and their nesting instincts coming into play. To both of them, it was a wholesome, safe, and comfortable feeling. They knew it intuitively. They both had searched a lifetime for a feeling like this.

Chapter 17

Having completed the weekend gig and made more money than she ever imagined she would, Julia made her way to the bus depot and got tickets for a round trip. Destination: Sausalito. It was Monday.

San Francisco was going through its usual calm kind of bustle. It wasn't the in-your-face bustle of New York City. It was a quiet, balanced kind of frenzy. White ambulances with blaring sirens were not snaking their way around yellow taxi cabs or anything like that. The business crowd milled about with an air of seriousness. Tourists strolled hand in hand or took pictures of each other standing in the middle of the sidewalk. It was as good a day as any to head out of town.

The bus was scheduled to depart at 9:30 A.M. Julia got on and sat for a while. Slowly, other passengers boarded the bus. There were not very many. Four couples, two women who could have been sisters or girlfriends, and one other man. Julia smiled to herself as she noted that women always outnumbered men, even when there was the smallest number of people present. The women on the bus had outnumbered the men by two. She wasn't factoring in the driver. She didn't know if it was going to be a man or a woman.

The bus was parked open when she arrived, and no one was in the driver's seat. Maybe there really were more women than men in the world. This was just one of the many curious little things that Julia always seemed to notice as she went about her life. Finally, the driver got on the bus. It was a man, but the men were still outnumbered, now only by one. He counted the people, checked his sheet, and asked the passengers about their destinations. There was no one getting off en route. It would be an easy run. Julia, the two women, and the four couples were all headed to Sausalito. The lone man said that he was going on to Muir Woods, and would change to a different bus in Sausalito. Julia wondered if he worked in the forests, or if he was just visiting; maybe hiking there over the next few days. He looked like the woodsy, outdoorsy, healthy, scruffy type. She leaned her head against the window and closed her eyes. She wanted to see the views along the way, but she was very tired. Since the driver was narrating the history of San Francisco and drawing the passengers' attention to landmarks and places of interest along the way, Julia thought it would be enough to just listen. She was really exhausted. Having danced all weekend was now kicking her butt. She hadn't felt the fatigue while she was dancing, but it was hitting her now. She knew she'd be making this trip again, so she'd have to catch the sights another time. She wanted to stay awake long enough to catch a glimpse of Alcatraz, which she knew was somewhere along that route, but she didn't know how far along the route, and her eyes and mind were already going into that blurry, twilight state, so she gave in to the fatigue. She was not aware of having slept throughout the entire ride, but now the driver was standing over her saying: "This is Sausalito, young lady. Last stop."

Sausalito was quaint and orderly; a sober-looking kind of place. Several elaborate yachts were docked in the Marina, and Julia wondered about their owners. Were they on board? If she bumped into one of them in the little gift shop nearby, would she recognize him or her as a wealthy boat owner? She walked into the gift shop and looked around. She'd buy herself a sweatshirt with Sausalito written on it. Maybe she would get the red one. They were 50% off. The navy ones were still full price. Why on earth? She figured that maybe the folks in that city were mostly Caucasians. They were not so inclined to wear red and orange, and colors like that. They basically wore navy, grey, or khaki things. Personally, she thought khaki was too close to their skin color, but they seemed to like it. She put the red shirt back, and took the navy one at full price to the counter. Her intention was not to stand out in that way. Her light skin and jet black hair gave her an exotic look, and that was quite enough. She would blend in with attire and attitude. Actually, she wanted people to take a second look at her. She would seem like one of them at first glance, but the second look would tell a different story and pique their interest. That second look was what she hoped for from the men, anyway. They say women dress for other women, but Julia didn't think that made any sense, and didn't think she should. What the hell would be the point of that? She knew she wouldn't want every man in that town, but she could have every man in that town wanting *her*. She could actually have her pick of the litter. As her mind played with these thoughts, Julia marveled at the way her instincts were leading her to tantalize and manipulate men. She hadn't seen her mother do that, and hadn't interacted with many other women, so she didn't know where it was all coming from. She just went with her inclinations, and so far everything was going her way. All the men she'd encountered thus far were willing to accommodate her in all kinds of ways. She was even thinking that "the little chicken" at that bank back in Paris would have pilfered Clayton's funds and given her as much money as she wanted, if she had insisted. She had let the plan fall through, not because she couldn't get it carried out, but because she had suddenly lost interest in the project. That was one of her flaws, if she could call it that, nothing held her interest for very long. She was ready to roll out of Paris the way she had rolled in; abruptly and spontaneously. She would go back to the States and live her own life. She was choosing California. It seemed to her that a girl could do anything there. As a child, she had visited San Francisco with Cora for a week, and had had a secret love affair with the place since then. She didn't really know why, but that city had just never left her mind. "Just like that song says," Julia thought half to herself, half out loud, "I left my heart in San Francisco." She would head there now and do her life. Her mother didn't have to know that she was back in the States. She didn't think she owed anyone, not even Cora, a rhyme or a reason for her actions. Cora would probably like to think that the two of them were close, but she, Julia, knew better. In her mind, nothing could be farther from the truth.

Chapter 18

The Big Payoff pulled into the Sausalito marina and docked. The crew had agreed that the captain's suicide had taken a toll on all of them, and that they needed to get on land and stay on land for a while.

After Gilbert's death they had continued their routines on the ship and maintained a semblance of normalcy, but somehow nothing and none of them was quite the same. Thelma seemed a little more at ease with the crew, but Clarence became quieter and more pensive than ever, and Ken was obviously in a state of grief and disbelief and overall depression. That kind of reconnecting with the soil could be therapeutic, Clarence eventually agreed, although at first he was not at all for it. They would stick around the West Coast for two months. They could travel around the state by self-driven rental cars if they had to; not that anyone of them felt comfortable driving. Traffic lights, corners, pedestrians, and those narrow pedestrian crossings could be the ultimate nuisance if not a downright danger to all involved. The whole land thing was a scary proposition, but they needed to take a break of some kind from the thoughts and moods they had all been caught up in those past few months, and since they didn't know what the fix for their predicament was, they were willing to just drop anchor somewhere, get off that boat, and be on solid ground for a while.

Meanwhile, Julia walked the streets of Sausalito, peeking into store windows and wondering about the people who owned the boats in the marina. She knew she wanted to hang around there to see who came and went, but maybe next time. This trip was about finding an inexpensive joint that she could stay in when she spent the weekends here. It would gradually become her second home, she'd get to know people, and she'd establish relationships with them and eventually find her way into their homes. They had to be living the good life. She could get a taste of it. She decided to walk back to the boutique where she'd bought the sweatshirt and purchase a baseball cap. She liked pulling her hair back when she wasn't working, and throwing on a baseball cap and some sun glasses. They made her feel dressed down and relaxed after the big flowing hair and layers of makeup that she wore for her patrons at *Babes*. The stuff she put on her lips to make them look pouty and sultry left them looking slightly swollen long after it was taken off, which was not exactly a bad thing. As a black girl she had full lips anyway, so this was just an enhancement. With the cap and glasses, all she put on her face was a thin layer of somebody's 30 SPF face cream, and she was ready to roll, or good to go, as older folks put it. Julia was ever mindful of the way people of her mother's generation expressed themselves, and in a strange way she resented being so much in their world. She felt the need to be out on her own and doing things a lot differently than life with Cora allowed, hence her decision to return to the States without her mother knowing and forge a life for herself in San Francisco. The people she had met so far, she thought were very cool. The proprietors of *Babes* were older men but they had mighty young attitudes, dressed in hip clothing, and used "with-it" teenage jargon. With their tight-fitting blue jeans, white shirts with sleeves rolled up at their elbows, collars opened down to their navels, and diamond-studded sunglasses, you couldn't tell by looking, or from the words coming out of their mouths, that they were over fifty. She had noticed, though, that they never used foul language. In a place like this, she expected people to be a little bit on the vulgar side. Of course, they all sported a perfect tan. Julia wondered if they actually went home to wives and children, and if they left home in the morning looking like that. Did they ever go to PTA meetings or do car pools? Did they wear other clothes when out with their families, or back to the first question, did they have families? She had really never spoken to any of them about anything other than her work schedule. She was content to wonder about it all and remain unknowing. She really didn't want to get to know them like that. She was going to dance, get paid, leave the joint, and have another life outside of there. She wasn't there to make friends. She just wanted to do what she now considered her job, do it well, and earn every dollar she could. The patrons were very happy with her, and tipped rather generously. This was a gig she could swing for a while.

Stepping out of the boutique now, having purchased her cap and put it on, Julia noticed a white man and a black woman walking toward one of the ships in the marina. Although they were together, Julia didn't think they were a couple. The woman was noticeably older than the man; not that that meant anything these days, she reminded herself. The woman's gaze met hers and for a few moments, neither blinked or looked away. The pair boarded the vessel. Julia read the words imprinted on the side of the ship: *The Big Payoff.* She made a mental note of it, and vowed to return later to try and meet that woman again. It was the only other black person she had seen in that town so far. Then it occurred to her that the boat might leave before she returned, so she decided to hang around for a few minutes to see if the woman would come out on deck, or something. Maybe she wanted to meet her, too. About three minutes into her wait, the woman appeared on the deck of the ship and called out to Julia.

"Hi, there."

"How are you?" Julia responded with a smile.

The woman was definitely older, and Julia thought she looked harmless enough.

"I'm fine. Where are you off to?"

"Oh, nowhere. I'm just visiting Sausalito. I work in San Francisco."

"Want to come in and have something cool to drink? The sun's kind of brutal today."

"Sure. Thanks. That sounds great."

With that, Julia began walking up the plank to the ship, thinking that she was beginning to meet people and possibly make new friends just as she had hoped. Maybe the woman had younger relatives that she would eventually meet. Wouldn't that be nice?

"Hi, again. I'm Thelma. The woman extended her hand which Julia enthusiastically took.

"I'm Julia. Nice of you to invite me in."

"This is home for me. I've worked on this ship for a while now."

"Oh, that's so cool."

"It's an okay job. I kind of stumbled into it. Nothing like this was ever in my plans when I was your age."

"But, Oh Gosh! That's so awesome!"

"That depends on how you look at it. So did you say you work in San Francisco?"

"Yes. I just started recently, actually."

"What do you do?"

"A little of this and a little of that. I'm just coming back from Paris, and I'm trying to get on my feet back here in the States."

"That's brave. You look to me to be still in your teens. Are your parents living?"

"Well, my dad I don't know much about. My mother lives here in the States, but I'm trying to be a grown-up and live on my own."

"Well, she must miss having you around."

"Oh, I don't think so. She's a very independent type. Her name is Cora. She doesn't even know I'm back from Paris."

Julia checked herself. She didn't know why she had divulged that last bit of information to a total stranger.

Thelma felt her heartbeat quicken at the sound of that name Cora again. She remembered a brief exchange she had had with Clarence one day when he told her that there were no coincidences in life; that the universe conspired to bring people and circumstances into your life as soon as you had that intent, consciously or not. As her mind began to formulate the next question, Ken, whom Julia had seen with Thelma a little bit earlier, joined them on deck. Thelma introduced him to Julia. He smiled at her warmly and offered his hand. Julia immediately felt that she wanted to get to know him better. Something about him felt *nice;* that was the only word she could think of in relation to him. She felt attracted to him, but it wasn't a lustful attraction. He was quite a bit older than she was, though not as old as Thelma. After all, all they had done was shake hands and smile at each other, and he was gone again.

"I'll catch you later." he said to Thelma as he walked away.

"It was nice to meet you, Julia. See you again."

"Same here," the young girl said smiling.

She also hoped that she would indeed see that man again.

Julia glanced at her watch and decided it was time to leave. She said farewell to Thelma, thanking her for letting her visit, and telling her that she hoped to visit again sometime.

"Well, we'll be here for a couple of months. We've all decided that we need a break from the ocean. There's someone else for you to meet, but we have to wait 'til he's out here and hanging about. He doesn't like being interrupted from whatever he's doing or thinking about, mostly thinking about, just to socialize. Not a people person, I suspect."

"Okay then. Thanks again, Thelma. Great meeting you."

"Bye, dear."

"Bye. Bye." Julia said and waved and smiled.

At *An Inn by the Sea* where Julia had booked a room for the two nights she was going to spend in Sausalito, she found that all she could think about was meeting the two people she'd met that day. She didn't wonder about the third one that she would meet at a later time. She had been immediately at ease with Thelma, and now she wondered why she hadn't told her the truth about her job in San Francisco, although she had shared the fact that her mother was unaware of her whereabouts. She had also felt some strange connection to Ken in that brief moment of their meeting. Maybe he felt like an old friend; she wasn't sure. Maybe he had the same personality as someone else she knew, but she couldn't think who that was. Not Clayton. Not Charlie. Not James. Not anyone she could call to mind. She showered and crawled in naked between the sheets. She slept soundly 'til 5:00 A.M. the next morning.

Chapter 19

Having heard the name Cora Jenkins from Ken, as they talked on the ship one day, and now the first name Cora again from this new girl, Julia, Thelma was beginning to put the thoughts that were running through her mind together like pieces of a puzzle. In fact, it didn't even seem like a puzzle. It seemed pretty obvious to her that Cora was the common thread between herself and Ken, and now, there was this Julia person adding herself to the mix. Thelma even thought she remembered thinking that Ken and Julia had exchanged a sort of penetrating gaze when they shook hands earlier; but that could have been her imagination. She was afraid of jumping to a conclusion prematurely. Maybe Julia was referring to a different Cora. She hadn't provided her mother's last name, and for some strange reason, Thelma had felt afraid to ask, so she let that opportunity to get more information slide. Really, what could be the chances of something like that happening? What could be the chance that she would run into her granddaughter shortly after wondering if her daughter had given birth to a child? It really just couldn't be, Thelma eventually convinced herself. She remembered Clarence's words that there were no coincidences in life again, but she blew them off.

Clarence came on deck just as Thelma was thinking about and struggling to negate that there was truth in any of the stuff he'd told her. He found his shipmate leaning on the railing just staring at the water.

"What's new, Mate?" He asked in a carefree tone, not seeming too interested in a response of any kind.

Thelma turned toward Clarence's voice and immediately turned back to face the water.

"Quite a bit." Thelma heard herself blurt out, and felt surprised by her own reply.

"So, what's new, Mate?" Clarence asked again. This time, with a chuckle, piqued interest, and a questioning look at Thelma. He moved closer to the woman and leaned on the railing next to her.

"Well, I just met a young lady."

"And?"

"She's in Sausalito for the weekend. Just ran into her as I was coming back from a walk around the area with Cheffy. I invited her in for a cool drink, and in conversation, she mentioned that her mother's name was Cora. Cheffy, our Ken, told me a little while back, about a relationship he had had with a woman named Cora Jenkins some years earlier. That woman is my daughter, but I didn't…"

"Your daughter?" asked Clarence, as a way of verifying what he thought he'd heard. As usual, he was suspending judgment, but he wanted clarity. He had never imagined Thelma with offspring.

"Yes. But I'll get back to that. I'm sure you want to know how I knew he was talking about my daughter and not some other Cora Jenkins, blah, blah, blah, but I knew from all the other circumstantial information and their ages, that he was talking about my daughter."

"Okay."

"So where was I? Oh! So I invite this girl in and she's telling me about having just come back to the States from Paris without letting her mother know, because she wants to be on her own, and she mentions that her mother's name is Cora.

"And?"

"And I'm looking at the girl and trying to picture my daughter at that age, which I can't really do because I gave her up for adoption the same day she was born. I have no idea what she looked like at that age, but I just had the weirdest feeling of being connected to this girl."

"So did you ask her to tell you more? I mean, about her mother?"

"No. I was afraid to, for one thing, I don't know why, and I also felt like I really knew and didn't need to ask."

"What did Ken say?"

"I haven't told him."

"Well, what are you going to do about all this?"

"I haven't decided. I'm just trying to piece things together."

"See, Thelma, that's what I mean about life, and letting all things be...not seeking revenge, not killing, not holding grudges, about not *doing* because we're all *being done*."

"Where are you going with this?"

"Well, that day you tried to talk to me about killing someone, I somehow knew you were referring to Ken."

"And you knew that how?"

"Who else could it be? Your real problem was with Gilbert, but he had already killed himself, and your target wasn't me. I knew that."

"And what makes you think I had a problem with Gilbert?"

"I knew from the total lack of communication between you two. Gilbert was always very friendly and social with women. You were the only woman on the ship, but you two never exchanged a word except it was work-related. You also never looked at him. You kept your eyes glued to your notepad while he spoke. I knew you two had to have some history between you. I wasn't born yesterday, but of course, I try to be non-judgmental about people's lives."

Thelma felt herself wanting to refute Clarence's assumptions. She could say it was the way she dealt with bosses, preferring to have only a professional relationship with them, but she knew he was right, and decided she might as well be truthful. After all, she really needed someone to talk to at this point. Besides, she had been thinking of giving up her life on the ocean lately. Maybe she could buy herself a small place and live out the rest of her days with her feet firmly planted on the ground. She had had no living expenses during all the years she worked on that ship, and had saved almost all of the money she earned.

"You're sort of right about Gilbert, but why would I want to kill Ken?"

"You tell me. I figure Ken won Gilbert's heart when you might have tried unsuccessfully."

"So you knew? About Ken and Gilbert?"

"No. I was born yesterday," Clarence said winking his left eye at Thelma and beginning a smile that didn't completely mature.

Thelma brought her hands up to her face, closed her eyes and rubbed them all the way out to the sides of her face as if smoothing out her temples. She felt some relief at having come clean with Clarence, not directly, but at least she hadn't denied anything he had surmised. Maybe she would talk to Ken about Cora again and tell him about her conversation with Julia.

"Life is such a bitch," Thelma whispered to the one quiet spot in her turbulent mind.

Chapter 20

Clayton was making plans for a wedding with Amy, having nothing at all to say to Cora. Not a call. Not a question. Not an explanation. Not a goodbye. *Nothing. Nothing.* He had finally found someone. They seemed a perfect fit. He couldn't believe he had spent all that time in a dead-end relationship, but he had no regrets. He also believed that nothing happened before its time, and he felt that he had grown in many aspects during the years he spent with Cora, so there were no regrets at all. In a strange way, she had prepared him for this love. It was a different time now. He was ready to move his life forward. In his heart he wished Cora the best. She deserved to be happy. Let her go and be happy. Done. Cora could hear his voice saying, "Let her be happy."

These last days Cora was in a different zone mentally. Trying to get revenge against Mike had taken a lot of her energy, and she didn't know what to do about Clayton. It was actually her fault that they were no longer a couple. She should have married him when she had the chance those first—it seemed—45 times. Her whole life seemed to have been lived pointlessly. Julia was the one good thing that had happened to her, but where was she these days? Cora had no idea. Her parents were gone now. She hadn't even formed "the ultimate girlfriend relationship." She felt unable to try again at loving another man. She had completely missed all of her boats. She had to continue working in order to occupy herself; that much she knew. She was sick of that, too, but she needed to continue doing it for a while yet. She would shut the door of her soul and focus on getting through the next few years of work so she could retire with a pension and health benefits. Imagine continuing to do something one was not that fond of doing anymore and having no other reason for doing it than to get health benefits eventually. What was the reason for living at all? She could chuck everything now and start a different life in a foreign country, learn a new language, live more light-heartedly, not caring so much about the future because she really didn't have one. She'd see. At this point it seemed easier to shut down and go on automatic pilot with the work situation. Get paid. Pay the bills. Close everyone out. Eventually die. She'd leave some papers in a vault at her bank and a note in her nightstand telling someone where to find them. That way, someone could notify her job in the event of her death, and know how to dispose of her body; seemed simple enough.

When Julia visited Thelma the next time, the two sat down on the deck of the ship, and Thelma vowed to get as much information as she could from the girl about her mother. First, she got Cora's last name and oh yes. It was Jenkins. She strategically gathered whatever information the young girl knew about her mother without giving anything away. Julia told Thelma about her mother's adoption at birth by a family whose last name was Jenkins. The family had already had two sons, so they were Cora's brothers by adoption, but her mother had only mentioned them once. Julia's discovery of her mother's diary one day revealed information about a relationship she had had with someone named Ken, no last name, who was her daughter's father. He didn't know about the baby; apparently

Cora had never told him she was pregnant, Julia went on. In her diary she had just spoken about it as *The Ken Fiasco*. Julia also told Thelma about being raped by her boyfriend, after which she ran off to Paris, convinced that her mother would never be there for her emotionally; hence her decision to cut all ties and live away from her now. Thelma did not blame either Cora or Julia for the present situation. She understood that everyone makes what they consider to be the best decision at the time. She, Thelma, had physically severed ties with Cora because she was unable to care for her, and gave her up for adoption, but she kept her daughter in her heart and prayed for her well-being every day; even as she hatched plans of revenge against her biological father. Cora had apparently severed emotional ties with Julia by not coming to her rescue when she needed her most. She had also deprived her of her father's love, never having even mentioned his name to her daughter. Julia might have sought him out, had she had the opportunity. Now Julia was severing ties with her mother in return. All of this pain was just going around in circles and duplicating itself.

Thelma felt that having Julia in her life as a friend now was a sort of healing thing. She didn't feel the need to let her know that she was her grandmother, but wanted the girl in her life. She, in turn, would just be there for her physically and emotionally; financially, too, if she needed that kind of support. In a convoluted back-handed sort of way, she would have her daughter back. They would form a friendship and a trust; that's all that mattered. Sometimes there are things that are better left unsaid. She had confided it all to Clarence who supported her decision and said that he intended to get back to the ocean with a different crew of people. He also supported Thelma's decision to buy a small condominium in Sausalito, and be there for Julia. He thought, though, that Thelma should let Ken in on the information, and let him choose his course of action.

Maybe he would want a relationship with Julia. As far as he knew, Ken had no family to speak of; having a daughter might be nice. Thelma did not agree. She didn't think Ken would want to be bothered at this late stage of the game. Clarence, in an uncharacteristic move, took it upon himself to let Ken know that he had a daughter alive and well in the world, and said that although he had made a point of not meddling in the affairs of others all his life, he felt compelled to offer Ken a chance at happiness again. Ken had given up Cora and lost Gilbert, and now there was a chance of starting to love all over again with his daughter. It was worth a shot.

Just as Thelma had predicted, Ken thought that there had been too much water under the proverbial bridge. He didn't ever want to be land-bound again anyway, so he had better not start anything with this girl. She seemed happy enough without him in her life. He didn't want to see her mother again either. What would be the point of that? He was sure he had hurt her when he left almost two decades ago. He had no interest in romantic liaisons with women anyway, or for that matter with anybody. He might have considered a friendship with Cora for Julia's sake, if the girl had been younger and still at home, but that was not the case. She was quite a grown-up, away from her mother, and creating a life for herself. Her chosen profession would not have been his choice for her, or advice to her, but hey….he hadn't had any say in her life or her decisions, hadn't even known of her existence until now, so what would be his role in her life?

Ken and Clarence would eventually pull up anchor and take to the ocean again, headed to God only knows where, each man keeping to himself; one of them always marveling at the blessed and fortunate circumstances of his life, the other being continuously pissed off about his.

Julia continued to be as happy as a clam, dancing through the weekend and on her days off, going to visit with Thelma, who was now staying in Sausalito permanently. She felt that this older woman was like another mother to her, and knew she was welcome in her home and heart. That was at once comforting and comfortable for her. Their visits grew more frequent, and their relationship became one of closeness and trust. They often just sat arm in arm on Thelma's sofa in the small condo and talked. Julia would sometimes lay her head on Thelma's shoulder and they would talk, about any and everything, and each felt comforted by the other. Julia had no inkling that she was in some way related to Thelma, and the older woman thought there was no point in divulging that piece of information; at least not at this point in time. Everything was perfect between them. Having her granddaughter in her life was like being given a second chance at having her daughter. Maybe the universe *was* beautiful and kind.

Julia was well aware of how young she still was, and that she needed a more mature and loving presence in her life. Thelma was providing that without micro-management and judgment. Julia felt totally accepted by the older woman, and in turn, began to love her in the same unconditional way. She was actually thinking that if Thelma should become frail when she was older and need someone to take care of her, that she, Julia, would be the one to do it—and willingly. In her heart she felt a kind of coming home, a kind of peacefulness about this new relationship.

The Final Chapter

Cora was now used to not having anyone around, and did not remember what she was initially thinking about as she sat in her room on the edge of her bed, but she was suddenly aware of an all-pervasive feeling of calmness and serenity. Her gaze came to rest on the Swarovski crystal Venus on the Half Shell that Mike had bought her for their first Christmas as a couple. Now, as she once again monitored her thinking, a practice that was now second nature to her, Cora realized that she had finally decided to let the whole Mike matter go. Looking back at the situations in her life that Mike knew about, and never participated in, she figured that he really never loved her at all. He wasn't there for her when she buried her parents, or her brother. He wasn't around for a lot of other important events in her life, and so she really hadn't lost his love. There is no way one could stand aside or so completely remove oneself from situations that affected a loved one so deeply. She clearly remembered that his comment to her at the news of one of those deaths was that "People live and then they die." She also remembered wondering what exactly he was made of. Through all those years they had been together, she had never found out, never known what his essence was. She needed to just get him out of her system once and for all. In fact, she knew that she had to forgive him for her own sake, S-O-B that he was, because the very thought of him was toxic to her spirit.

Cora had also been told by a girlfriend of hers that she shouldn't feel that Mike's rejection of her had much to do with her; that it had more to do with the fact that he needed, in this society, to marry a white woman. If he married a black woman, he had to worry about how his folks would feel, what his friends would think, what his co-workers would say, how even total strangers on the goddamned street would judge him. It would be a rough life for him unless he grew the cahones of an elephant, which in reality, he was simply unable to do. Then there would be the issue of children; another potentially nightmare situation. Tyra had just had a show with mixed-race children talking about emotional scarring, suffered from the intolerance of others, and their own emotional confusion. Some of them felt they had to choose sides; some felt disdain for one or other of their parents; they couldn't even check a box on a form that asked about ethnicity without thought. Not an easy life! A burning shame in America in the twenty-first century, but a reality all the same.

Cora knew that letting go of this issue was a good decision on her part, but didn't know how she'd gotten there. She still wasn't sure it was all of the reasoning with her of friends who meant well.

When that concept of forgiveness was first introduced to her by some sage or spiritualist, either on television or in a book, she thought it was ridiculous, if not downright impossible. Now, suddenly, she was at that place. She wondered how her life and her daughter's would have turned out if she had gotten to that place sooner. Julia was totally gone from her life now. Cora reflected on her earlier decision to shut herself off from the world and life, to continue working just to stay alive, and then die alone. Bad idea! No way in hell would she allow anyone to negatively influence her life like that. Just because Mike didn't realize how precious she was, didn't mean she wasn't precious and worthy of all things good—of happiness in life; just like atheists cannot take away the existence of God by simply not believing, he could not discard her worth by simply not recognizing it. She had cast pearls before swine; no reflection on her or the pearls that the swine did not see them for what they were or know what the heck to do with them.

Cora now recalled that this had always been one of Mike's rhetorical questions to her: What am I going to do with you? Obviously, the answer was supposed to be *Nothing,* but she guessed that neither one of them knew it at the time, and it was left unanswered; waiting instead to be played out.

The sages had often explained that holding on to anger and resentment created low vibrations for the soul, and were therefore an impediment to enlightenment and evolution. Someone else had described it as drinking poison and waiting for the other person to die. That aspect, the poisoning piece, she realized back then, might have been a plausible or feasible one, but Cora reasoned that she didn't exactly know where her soul was in its evolutionary process, anyway, so what was the difference? Was that whole process going on now, or had some things been already worked on in a previous incarnation? There was a drawback to not having easy access to information from previous lives, if there had been any, Cora thought, and she wasn't big on the idea of past-life regression through a medium. Some cans of worms were better left unopened! Life was probably just one big karmic cycle anyway, with each action creating some new karmic debt to be repaid. No one knew for sure. It could be that she would come back as a dog, and get adopted again; a ridiculous thought to be sure, but that was Cora; always the ridiculous side of her brain trying to edge the sublime side over—just a smidgen.

Cora also realized, as she looked at where she'd been emotionally and where she was now, that forgiveness was not something that could happen before the time was right, so she did not beat herself up about holding on to her anger that long. Nothing happened before its time. That, she believed. Was it the passage of years that had brought this awakening? Did age actually bring reason, as the old folks had promised they would? Was it her many years of therapy? In therapy, she had never discussed the relationship with Mike, per se, although she had mentioned it in her first session as one of the relationships that she had deeply cared about and lost. Maybe the matters that she did discuss and resolve were somehow tied to it, and resolving them had helped to resolve it. She wasn't sure. She also knew that it wasn't because she had found the love that some say heals all wounds, and she certainly had not found religion which the fanatics say, guarantees perfect peace. Any one of these reasons, or any combination of them would have been a recipe for the surrender and serenity she was experiencing now, but she knew it wasn't any of those. Whatever the reason, Cora was now willing to reside in that place of forgiveness and peace, and move forward with her life and herself. The willingness to do that made her feel physically better, too. She actually felt a lightness in her stomach. That spot in the middle of her ribcage which always felt heavy, somewhat blocked, and even a little sore, now felt pain-free, clear and open. She deeply hoped that this feeling was not a temporary one. She had let go of resentment about other matters in the past, or so she thought, only to pick them up again when something new reminded her of the experience. That was not a good thing. She had to be sure there was no residue to be stirred up again. In the case of the issue of Mike which she seemed always to be focused on, Cora now knew that she was the only one in the game, but then again, as far as that game was concerned, she had *always* been the only one in the game, so there was nothing new here. Mike had completely moved on with his life. In fact, the last report she had of him had brought home that fact. The same mutual friend who had first broken the news of his marriage, had run into him at a retirement party for someone they both knew, and he had not so much as asked if she was, by chance, still in touch with Cora. The news had sent a lightning bolt through her heart again, and she realized that she could not live the rest of her life like this, always trying to gather news about him, always hoping she was somehow on his mind, and being disappointed. Actually, he was not the type to keep people on his mind. She never really thought that he had any allegiance to anyone. When he lost friendships, he never spoke of them or thought of them. He was impatient with his mother when she became ill, and needed his attention. He was usually mostly self-serving. You know what? Cora now suddenly realized, Mike was really *not* a very nice person. Handsome is as handsome does. She heard herself call him a son of a bitch again, out loud this time, and started to monitor her thoughts. She thought it curious that he had attended the party alone, and did not wear a wedding band, (as she had found a way to find out), but Cora remembered that he was never one for jewelry of any kind, not even a watch. He was one of the most casual and conservative men when it came to his mode of dress. As for being alone, maybe his wife had had a previous engagement, or was pregnant and just not up to being social. He would be leaving the party early, as he was wont to do, and hurrying home to her. He would tell her how happy he was that he had her to come home to. Cora remembered the times when they had both left social gatherings early to be alone together. Was she ever going to free herself of memories from that relationship? As she asked herself that question, she realized how strange it was that she had hurt for such a long time, or why she had even thought that her decision to leave when she did was wrong, because when she told her story to friends, even without details, the first remark out of their mouths was always that they couldn't believe she had stayed with him that long. To them the wrongness of the relationship was as clear as day. She, however, always thought it was okay.

Cora was fully aware that she was not rummaging through that garbage heap of thoughts because she was back there with them, but rather as a way of ensuring that she had waded through that garbage heap of a relationship, and was now safely on the other side of it; so far away from it now that she could no longer smell its stench. As she sat amidst these thoughts and feelings she stretched her hand out and looked at her still-bare, left, ring-finger. It was the one finger on which she never wore a ring. In a strange way, she felt that she was holding that finger in reserve for a wedding band. She hadn't managed to save her virginity for Mr. Right, but that wedding finger was sacred. Cora noticed that she was laughing at herself again.

She felt now that the relationship was destined to end the way it did. There was no way that Mike and she could have continued to engage in that pretentious and dishonest relationship. His feelings of uncertainty and displays of rejection might have been more blatant than hers, but she also had issues that did not help or foster intimacy. She had dated him at the worst period of her life, though all seemed well. People close to her were coming apart at the seams, and she had been saddened, anxious, vulnerable, and embarrassed. She had never discussed these matters with Mike, and so, while he hid her from his family, she hid her family from him, and they were both engaged in a conspiracy of sorts. Had she been fully in the relationship with only their future to think about, had she felt better about herself during those times, things might have turned out differently. Her deepest fear was that he could not love her if he knew the truth about her life. Not that there was anything disgraceful going on. Her family issues were related to addiction and fragile mental states; veritable illnesses which should have been looked at as such. No one had committed murder, or gone to prison for acts of dishonesty or violence. No Mansons or Madoffs in the mix. In fact, when the various illnesses were under control, there were no better or more brilliant people you could meet. However, Cora felt it necessary to hold up a false front that she thought he could love better. Mike's not committing to a serious relationship allowed her to hide what she felt she needed to hide, especially since she knew he could be very judgmental about people. In one of her attempts to open up to him about a matter concerning one of her brothers, he had made the comment that it would be pathetic if she turned out to be the sanest member of her family. That did not sit well with her, and she knew she could never bare her soul to him the way people do in intimate, supportive relationships, so she continued to live with her disguise. He was not a nice man. Cora wondered if telling him the truth about her situation and the fact that she was doing everything in her power every single day to straighten out the mess and set the afflicted family members back on their feet, maybe—just maybe—would have gotten her his love—problems and all. Even then it was still *maybe* because she had seen his reaction to milder things, even in his own family, and it wasn't encouraging.

She knew from the self-help books she read that people were perceived by others the way that they perceived themselves. She had perceived herself as strong but in some way substandard, accomplished but without self-confidence, and worthy yet inferior. She might have radiated those messages out to the subconscious mind of the person in that relationship with her (*she wouldn't even call him by name now*), hence his feelings of ambivalence about her. He liked her but not enough, wanted her but didn't want her, kept the relationship going, but wouldn't commit.

Now, however, there was no going back to fix anything about the way they had lived that relationship, and she had now let it go forever.

While Cora conversed with herself in that manner, she reflected on her thoughts, and verified that she was not once again heaping blame on herself the way she always did when things didn't turn out right. No. She knew that in every situation, it took two to tango. If she had perceived him as kind and compassionate, she might have felt safe enough to be open. There were people she knew less intimately that she was able to tell about the issues she dealt with every day that caused her pain, anxiety, and embarrassment, and diminished her feeling of self-worth. Cora thought that *he* didn't see through her well enough to determine that she lived with a disguise, but again, you couldn't underestimate that male radar! It was probably just all in a feeling that he got. What he hid from her about his family, she didn't quite know either. There was something about a stepsister who was on the skids, and a stepbrother whom no one had heard from in years, but there were the girl cousins, as he referred to them, who did well, and who were his pride and joy. An uncle had also been a lawyer, and there were the relatives who were educators that he always talked about. All of his family members seemed better than the family members Cora had to talk about, at least on the surface.

That wasn't quite true. Her dad had been a scholar, an upstanding gentleman, musician, and historian. He was well loved for his kindness to many members of his community, and had produced many literary works. Her mother, formerly a schoolteacher, was a reserved and classy woman; the epitome of decency and high integrity. Her oldest brother had even been awarded an MBE title (Member of the British Empire) by the Queen of England for outstanding contributions to communities in London, another brother was a successful plumber/electrician type who considered himself a metaphysician, and the family had been generally well-respected in their circles. But somehow, all of a sudden, things had changed for them when one of the sons began suffering from a spate of nervous breakdowns, and another, who was originally a member of the clergy, became alcoholic. The ill fate of the two brothers was Cora's focus and the undoing of her self-esteem. All the positive aspects of her life faded into the background, and she felt that these unfortunate circumstances were now the family's legacy; she felt worthless. It didn't help that she also carried the financial burdens of the family since her father died, and their home and business went up in flames about three months later. All these things had happened a few months before meeting *him,* and so she got in with him in the throes of her woes. Maybe she should have shared her story right at the start, and let him decide whether or not to be friends with her, since that was the way their quasi love story began—as friends-and she was calling it quasi because, in retrospect— there was not enough love in his heart to make a love story. There is not enough love to make a love story if only one person is in love. Pie shell with no apples doth not an apple pie make.

Of course, one could wonder and wonder what if, so Cora was glad she had finally let it all go. In life's matters, you make the best decision you can make at the time. Things come out the way they come out. Cora liked to say that, "life tumbled out at you."

When she said that, she always had the visual of a cornucopia—the type you see at Thanksgiving—filled to the brim and overflowing— falling to the floor and spilling its contents. She felt that life in its fullness sometimes slipped out of your hands and fell to the floor, causing all kinds of things, some you liked and some you didn't like, to tumble out and fall to the ground, rolling around you in all directions. Some items you would gather up; some items you would lose. Along with letting go of that relationship mess, as she now saw it, Cora decided to look at her life in a "kinder, gentler" manner, to quote a past President. If it was all about the intention, as Cora believed, and not the actual outcome, then she had nothing to blame herself for. This whole scheme to make *him* pay had been her only "evil" intent, and she was now done with that endeavor. All else was mere happenstance.

As her thought-monitoring continued, Cora took herself back to the other major agony-causing issue in her life. For years she had blamed herself for her brother's death, believing as she did, that if she had been more tolerant of his drinking, knowing that it was an illness, and more patient with him in terms of his beginning to be a responsible adult, he would not have begun that last bout of drinking which eventually led to his death by drowning. She was allowing him to stay with her for a while with the good intention of getting him to turn his life around. He was probably making every effort, but she was eager and a little impatient because things were not exactly working. She was becoming uncomfortable with his presence around her because of the way he carried himself in an environment where she was pretty much respected. In addition, they were in cramped quarters. There was just not enough physical space for two adults. She had to hide him from that person, too. Anyway, she was trying to make the best of a bad situation until the night he went out to the supermarket and didn't return until the next day. The friend that he went out with had called in the middle of the night to say that he was going home to his family, because her brother had gone to a woman's house and he couldn't wait for him to take him home. Her brother called the next morning expecting her to pick him up. She didn't. He eventually came home and went straight to bed. When the friend had called earlier, he had told Cora that her brother had had a drink. The news sent her into a panic knowing what she knew about his drinking spells. There was no way she could cope with it. In her panic and anger and fear of being unable to handle what would follow, she didn't even ask a question when he showed up at the house that Sunday morning after spending the night out. The grocery store run had become an entire night out. He had returned with no groceries, but that was not even the problem. It wasn't even a problem that he had shown disregard for the fact that she was expecting him back several hours earlier, and had been worried sick. It was about the fear of being unable to go looking for him on the street if he decided to get really drunk for several weeks, because that's how long his drinking spells ran before they subsided into a kind of groggy sobriety. It was the fear of his getting into trouble with the law for wandering the streets in an unruly fashion, talking to strangers, trying to joke around with dangerous types. When he drank he became a different person, one that was fearless and reckless. It was also the fear of having to leave him drunk in the house when she went to work, not knowing what would happen to the house or to him.

She looked at him lying in a fetal position, not having said a single word to her when he walked in, flew into a blue rage and told him he had to find his own place to live right away. They had been talking about his moving out anyway, and they both had been trying to find him a place, but things had gotten out of hand now, and she needed to have him out of her house sooner rather than later. She went back to her bedroom, and when she came out again, he was gone. She yanked his clothes out of the closet and put them on a chair. He had left again without saying anything to her. He really had to go. He returned several hours later, took his things and said he was leaving. By then her anger had cooled, and she told him he could stay until he had a place, but he refused. He said he would sleep in the subway. She couldn't make him stay, and she worried about him the rest of the night. The next day, she received a call from a distant cousin of theirs saying that he was with him. Several days later, the cousin called again to say that her brother was acting strangely, not taking showers, and just making him generally uncomfortable in his own house. He had gone out without leaving word of his whereabouts, and this cousin was unwilling to let him back in the house.

That night, Cora went to get him. She had to wait a long time because he wasn't there when she got there. Eventually he arrived, looking intoxicated. He said it was because he hadn't slept. She remembered taking him back to her place in the back of her car, and waiting until one of her neighbors was out of sight before ushering him out of the car and quickly into the house. She couldn't let anyone see him, or her. He was in a disheveled state, and she was as angry as hell. She found it all so very stressful. Within the next several hours she made arrangements to get him into a hospital for detoxification. That was another long process, another story for another time. After she left, he wound up leaving the hospital and wandering the streets. A co-worker that she trusted and told what was happening went with her to look for him. They found him in the hospital cafeteria trying to buy something to eat, but he had only a dollar or two in his pocket. They took him home. She struggled to get him in the shower and to sober him up amidst tears and a feeling of utter desperation. Yes, she had to get him into the shower first, because she had one of those noses, and that had been another one of the problems living with him in a small apartment. Over the next few days, somehow, she was able to convince him that he needed help, and he checked into another hospital. Cora breathed a sigh of relief. She was sure that things would start improving now, but she was wrong. He was released from the hospital one day before she expected him, and instead of coming home, he took himself to the first open bar. He called her from there at about two in the morning to say he would be home the next morning. She volunteered to go pick up him up, but he refused to let her. She waited all day. About five o'clock that evening she had a call from the police saying that he was at the precinct because he had an open alcoholic beverage on the street and no identification. They had checked as far as they could, and wanted some information from her. Since her information matched what he had told them, and he had never been in trouble with the law, they volunteered to put him on the train and send him home. Cora knew that they had been nice to him because he was such an impressive speaker, with a deep, rich tone, a British accent, perfect grammar, and a winning smile. He also had a very charming way of interacting with people. Some of the same neighbors she was desperately trying to hide him from had met him somehow in the complex, and had told her what a wonderful brother she had. In fact, he had even given away her batteries to the people next door, because they needed some right then and there, and he didn't think they should trouble themselves with going to the store just to pick up batteries when his sister had some lying around. They could replace them later, or not.

Cora had been so shaken up by the call that she called *him*, her then paramour, on the phone and told him. He did not have a major reaction at the time, but he did bring it up several months later as an awful thing that had somehow stained her in his sight.

At about ten o'clock that night, her brother showed up at the house with a cab driver and told her that she needed to pay the fifteen-dollar fare. Cora paid the money, and ordered her brother out of her house again. If he didn't live there, she would not have to deal with these things. She really could not live like this. She spoke to the A.A. people. They advised her to put him out of her house and let him be. Having him with her was probably enabling the whole situation. He had been enabled all along, first by their parents, then by his wife, then by his former colleagues and bosses, and now by her. Over the years, everyone in his life had made excuses for him, paid his bills, covered his tracks, forgiven him, and given him second, third, and fourth chances. That Sunday, the friend who had taken him to the grocery store some days earlier found him and took him to Cora's. She didn't let him in. On the Monday that followed, however, the weather turned ugly, and Cora fearing that her brother would be caught outdoors in a storm, got in her car and drove around the city 'til she found him, and took him home again. By now, it was early December. The struggle to keep her brother at home, keep him sober, monitor his whereabouts when he was not at home, deal with his not showering or keeping himself clean, was all an uphill battle. He left the house sometime around December 20 with another friend, and that friend called to say he had dropped him off somewhere. He wasn't heard from until December 26th. Meanwhile, Cora worried. She knew he was not exactly missing, but she had no idea where he was. On December 26, he came back to Cora's. She somehow talked him into returning to the Caribbean where he had lived before coming to Cora's, since things were not working out for him at the time. Maybe he could stay there the rest of the winter and return to her in the spring. On December 27th, he took himself back there. Cora felt relieved, thinking he'd be safer there, would have some time to rethink things. It would also give her a breather, and she could probably try again after he had been away and had some time to gain a different perspective on the whole concept of treatment and sobriety. On the morning of his departure, her brother began to get himself drunk at the airport while they waited for his flight to board. A friend of Cora's had accompanied them. Their appeal to the waitress at the bar not to serve him any more alcohol was ignored. Cora was told that her brother was an adult. The waitress did not respond to the gentleman with her, or even make eye contact with him. Her brother got to his destination drunk, and continued to drink. He ended up in the hospital with major injuries from a fall. A few days later, he tried to walk out of the hospital. He was stopped and returned to bed. Later that night he tried to escape via a back window that opened onto the ocean. It was now February 18th. It was pitch black out. It was the middle of the night. No one saw him try to leave this time.

He fell into the ocean and drowned.

His body was found four days later, still dressed in the hospital gown, a bruise on his forehead. He was floating face down, arms outstretched. His eyes had not been plucked out of his head by birds. Thank God. A biblical verse about God not letting the eyes of his own be plucked from their heads by birds was moving around vaguely in her mind, but she couldn't recall it exactly. Her brother had been a priest at one point in his life. Maybe he was still favored by the Father despite his human frailties. Maybe it was true that God forgives us everything.

When that detail of her brother's death was revealed to Cora several days later, she knew that he was attempting to swim, but between the withdrawal symptoms, the injuries from the fall, a troublesome heart, the blackness of the night, and a heavy tide, he couldn't do it. Her grief was all the more.

Somewhere in Cora's mind, she knew that she had killed her brother. Had she not lost patience with him, had she kept him by her side, had she not put pressure on him to find his own place and stand on his own two feet, he would not have started that last bout of drinking that led to his death, and he would be alive today. It didn't matter than he had embarked on bouts of drinking when she had had no say in his life.—had not "set him off." It didn't matter that he had died in another country far away from her. It didn't matter that they were only two years apart in age, and that he was an adult who should be responsible for himself. It didn't matter that he was as stubborn as a mule, and no one could tell him what to do. None of that mattered. What mattered to Cora was the fact that she had been a bad sister; selfish and impatient; unwilling to share her space with someone who obviously needed help. Yes, she had opened her doors to him initially, but she should have known that 'curing' an alcoholic was a long-term deal, and she should have committed herself to doing all or nothing. Somehow she had failed him, and she could not forgive herself. *He* advised her to write down the sequence of events leading up to her brother's death, and try to see how she had tried to help him; try to see that she had no blame in this whole thing, but it didn't work. Cora would eventually see a therapist in an effort to resolve the matter with herself, and eventually quit therapy because the pain of her guilt was not subsiding. She also knew during the course of that therapy, without the issue even being brought up, that she was being overly sympathetic to another family member, and was most likely overcompensating for what she perceived to be her hand in the death of the brother who had died. How many demons could she live with? Wasn't it time to give herself a break? It seemed like she had put several nooses around her own neck wondering which one would actually hang her; cut off her air supply and finally kill her.

Deciding to let the relationship issue go was part of Cora's decision to let everything go. All of her mistakes needed to bite the dust and go away forever. All of them: The ones that related to her relatives and lovers, and the ones that related to herself. All of her intentions had been good. Mistakes had been made along the way, perhaps, but all her intentions had been good. Being human, mistakes were just a part of life. People make what they perceive to be the best decisions at the time. Cora believed that no one actually chose to make the wrong decision. No one, she thought, actually sets himself or herself up to repay karmic debt. That belief probably did not extend to felons who made decisions about breaking laws and committing crime; she didn't know for sure. She was really just referring to regular people who were simply in the process of living a life. Cora knew that she was as good as anyone else. She had accomplished much by herself, and had a devotion to family that even her closest friends did not understand. In addition, she had an acute sense of fairness, good will towards all people, and a wide open heart. She was letting these attributes go to sleep in her consciousness, consumed as she was by grief and sadness. She just had to let it go. She knew she would do better in the next phase, because this present pain was having a strangely cleansing effect on her spirit.

The pain burned fiercely, but somewhere underneath these red-hot flames and pungent fumes, Cora recognized a purifying fire, and she envisioned herself as a phoenix rising out of the dust and ash. She thought of the ancient mariner, and remembered that she felt as light and free as he, the mariner, was reported to have felt when he finally got rid of that goddamned bird; yes, the albatross. That was when she first walked away from him. In those first months, she felt as though the albatross had finally been removed from around her neck. It had been weighing her down for years, and she moved with lightness in her step now. Her pain in regard to that relationship had only come when she saw how easily he had moved on without looking back, and found himself a permanent relationship in one-third of the time that he had spent with her. It was then that she started wondering which aspect of herself was not good enough.

Mike had spent every day of all those years pulling her in and then pushing her away. Push, Pull, Push, Pull, Push, Pull; and then one Sunday in a phone conversation, Push, Push. His actual words were neither push nor pull; they were words that could have been either in their sound to the ear, but they were in their sentiment and intention a major Push, and there was no mistaking it. Cora took the hint, made the decision, and stood in solidarity with herself. She would not betray her spirit any longer.

Out of the romance wilderness now, Cora was deciding, on her own, to take her life back unto herself. She would put aside the issue of her brother's death; that would be guilt done with. She would let go of her desire to get even with Mike and stop beating herself up for poor decisions she had made at different times in her life; that would be regret done with. She would forgive her mother for not protecting her that time from being molested by a family friend, and for insulting her that other time when she told her that she wanted a green dress. On that day she stopped liking the color green (she didn't extend that to trees, but she never bought herself another green thing, and she remembered the incident every time she saw green items or someone wearing that color); that would be anger done with. She would forgive her father for not loving her unconditionally (She knew that she needed to be smart in school and pretty-looking to gain his approval, and approval somehow translated to love); that would be resentment done with. Cora knew that ridding herself of these little life-issues would not cover all the ground she needed to cover and cleanse, but it would move her a long way forward, and in the right direction.

Part of the problem was that Cora seemed like a perfectly happy, successful, normal person. Her life was not a screaming success, meaning that everyone in the world knew her by one name like Cher, or Madonna, or Oprah. Nor was she even a two-name wonder like Maya Angelou, or Tina Turner, (all of whom were women she considered phenomenal for one reason or another), but she was far from being unsuccessful; definitely not on the skids. She had her own home and a great job that she really enjoyed, along with a couple of degrees and several certifications. She could add many letters after her name, if she chose to. She bought whatever she wanted and traveled where and when she pleased. A girlfriend had once said to her: "Girl, you do some serious traveling!" She was considered widely traveled, highly educated, well read, and eloquent in her circles. No one would think of her as needing pity. Her friends thought she laughed a lot, and was quite funny. Her happiness and self-esteem quotients had to be in the superior range. Everyone was wrong.

Cora knew she also had to change the way she handled her aloneness, now that Clayton was no longer a part of her life, he had moved on to someone else, and she was without any male companionship. She still bought herself nice things, but she would catalog shop; and although she bought designer things, she really never flaunted a name or sported a logo. She just knew the cut or the quality was there. She noticed, though, she had become less self confident and easy as she became more and more consumed with the idea of getting even with Mike. There were stores she now avoided entering by herself, although she didn't think that was so much of a self-esteem issue, as it was the idea that they could see she wasn't draped in fur and wearing platinum and diamond jewelry, and some of these high-end stores were snooty like that.

Cora was usually content to buy the best that she could afford, without going overboard or all the way, because while she was well off, she was not exactly a Getty or a Rockefeller, and she also didn't feel a need to be always so gussied up. She had a girlfriend who was like that. Jenny was always dressed to the nines, even for trips to the market. She would do faux fur and platinum-clad sterling, or even simulated diamond jewelry and get away with it because she carried herself with a certain poise and grace; had a kind of rich air to her demeanor. Cora just wasn't one for faking stuff like that. Her big thing was having a beautiful living space, especially since she spent a lot of time at home. A camper, she was not. She thought it was enough that she had to feign emotional well-being. How much work was a girl supposed to do if she had to leave the privacy of her home where she lived alone; leave the comfort level of her own company and venture into the judgmental arena of co-workers, shopkeepers, museum curators, and restaurant owners? She would just go to the places she could handle without much ado. She did go to the theatre by herself quite a bit, and that was somewhat uncomfortable initially, but bearable once the show began. The trick was to arrive just as the show was starting, and make a quick entrance into the half-lit room as the lights were going down. The timing had to be impeccable. Thank goodness these things usually started on time, so she could actually keep an eye on the second hand of her watch, and arrive just at the crucial moment. Standing out in the lobby alone while other theatergoers were in pairs or groups was a definite no-no. She'd made that mistake once, and boy, those doors couldn't open soon enough. That night she glimpsed a guy who was lone-ranging it like herself, and he was literally hiding behind a pillar. She was braver than that. She stood out in the open, but close to one of the door people, and talked about how cold it was outside, all the while praying that the lady would ask her if she wanted to be seated early. It didn't happen. From time to time Cora cast a furtive glance toward the door, as if expecting her party to arrive at any moment. Why couldn't she allow herself to feel and look as alone as she really was? Maybe her fellow lone-ranger guy behind the pillar would have spoken to her if he thought she was indeed alone, but she looked as though she were expecting someone. That night, Cora decided that standing alone in a theatre lobby was something she was never doing again! (It was weird how one uncomfortable incident on one occasion could get her to make a decision about the way she would handle similar occasions the rest of her life). Once inside, it got a little easier. A female usher seemed greatly admiring of the fact that she dared dress up and come alone. Of course, she couldn't voice that thought, it would have been most inappropriate, but women read each other well. Had it been a male usher, he might have been thinking, "Gee! She has no man, I wonder what's wrong with her." And she would have been able to read that, too, but she wouldn't be as certain. Cora believed at that point in her thinking that she had two thoughts about the way men felt about her. Either they didn't like her that much, or as more than a casual friend, or they really liked her now, but wouldn't like her later. She always thought of a man's romantic love for her as something that would wane rather than grow deeper over time. She couldn't exactly pinpoint where that idea had come from. Then again, maybe she could, but was unwilling to delve into that now. The mind had a way of letting you know when to put the cap on pain. Cora chuckled to herself, better denial than Alzheimer's. The former was at least voluntarily reversible.

All these issues reflected on, taken into consideration, and decided upon, made for a turning point in Cora's spirit. She realized that the first step would have to be either a decision to think differently, or decide differently about her thinking; maybe she would have to do both. Guilt, regret, anger, and resentment, all of which had become friends and established close-knit, binding relationships with her, would have to go out the door—and immediately. They would just have to walk out, leave, never to return. A couple of them, she knew, would try to beg their way back into her life, but she would just have to say no. She knew she would have to remind herself of her resolve to shake sadness off every day for a while. After all, the crud had built up over the decades of her life. She probably could not just flush it out in one fell thought, although she felt that she had done just that. She might have to write her resolve on her bathroom mirror where she could see it every morning and every night, and keep a copy in her purse, but she would do whatever it took to break free. Today she resolved that compassion for self would replace guilt.

Forgiveness would replace bitterness and anger and their accompanying need for revenge. Love would replace regret, and understanding would replace resentment. She might even try to buy into that favorite idea of many that "it is better to have loved and lost, than not to have loved at all." Yeah! Right! Tell that to an aching heart. However, she would do her best—in fact, she was determined—to chart a new course for herself without the companionship of those four nasty enemies: Regret, Guilt, Anger and Fear, who had hypocritically posed as intimate friends over her decades of living. She didn't want their help anymore; (and she was sure they had faithfully and loyally helped her to have a life devoid of true happiness and deep romantic love, among other things).

Cora felt that the knot in the middle of her ribcage had come undone, and she had an intense sense in her spirit of being very collected and focused; very free. She was suddenly and strangely aware of being actually—she was afraid to say it—happy. She walked to the front door and lifted the lid of the mailbox. There was nothing there. Maybe the mail hadn't come yet. She looked at her car still parked in the driveway. She hadn't bothered to put it in the garage. She liked being able to spontaneously hop into the car and leave, without having to open that clangy garage door. For some reason she had resisted buying an electronic garage door opener. Her consequence for that decision was hoisting up that clangy thing to get out of the garage, and hauling it back down when she got out. Besides, the door had this way of slowly ascending in an almost ceremonious manner; or like a slow yawn. Then there was the backing out, first to the left, then straight back with her neck at that weird angle. These little processes slowed her down, took the spontaneous edge off her movements. She imagined that the gates of heaven would open something like that—very slowly—and she envisioned the angel in charge trying to decide if she had been good on earth, and now deserved to be let in. Cora knew that her Catholic mother would not be pleased with her if she knew what was going on in her head. She had always accused her of being a little irreverent; slightly blasphemous.

Cora decided she would run out for a while. She would make a trip to Neiman Marcus. She loved that store. She grabbed her Peggy Guggenheim sunglasses; they were her favorite pair. She thought they gave her an elegant and stylish flair. Today, she would buy herself a green silk dress. She had seen a great one made by Hengst—knee length, wrap style under the waistline, bare shoulders, youthful looking without being inappropriate for her age. Several stores in her area carried the line. She was sure she could find it. Maybe she would try Anabelle's Boutique first. She could wear it to Clayton's wedding in another couple of months, if she decided to attend.

Clayton had sent invitations to Julia and Cora. The invitations had been sent separately and allowed for each of them to bring an escort. Why was Clayton assuming that she had already moved on? Or maybe he wasn't assuming that. Being Mr. Good Manners, he must have just thought it was the right thing to do. At that point, Cora checked in with herself to see how she felt about losing Clayton to another woman, after having had him to herself for so many years. She needed to know how she felt about losing one more relationship. She was surprised to discover that it was neither here nor there with her.

And then…

Clayton's wedding day came. Cora looked great in the emerald green dress. She wore silver shoes and carried a medium size, silver clutch. God only knew where in the world Julia was. Cora went to the wedding alone. She walked in and sat in the first seat of the seventh pew on the side of the church that was reserved for Clayton's guests. The satin bows at the ends of each row of pews throughout the church gave a feeling of opulence to the place. The flowers on the altar were exquisite. The wedding ceremony was beautiful. Vows were exchanged that the two had obviously written themselves for one another. Cora didn't know Amy, but she could hear Clayton's heart in the words he had written for his bride. After the priest pronounced the couple man and wife, and the groom had kissed the bride, the couple received a final blessing, and the congregation applauded. Clayton and his wife began their walk down the aisle, smiling happily at their loved ones who had gathered together for their special day. The organist played the Ave Maria with full swell. An aura of bliss was present.

In one easy fluid movement, Cora pulled a silver handgun out of her purse and pumped a single bullet directly into Clayton's chest just as he reached her pew. The second bullet went into the bride as Clayton clutched his chest and collapsed onto the floor. People began scrambling all over the church, some toward the couple, some toward the sanctuary, some of them toward the door of the church, in an effort to escape the mayhem. The killer stood motionless, still clutching the weapon. No one looked in Cora's direction, or came near her.

After what seemed an eternity of absolute chaos and helter skelter, the ambulance arrived to take the two bodies away. The police showed up, too, took the gun out of Cora's hand, and put handcuffs on her as they read her rights and began escorting her out of the church. Cora did not resist arrest. As she walked calmly out of the church between the two lanky policemen she thought about her life. Her adoptive parents were dead; her biological parents she had never met, her daughter had abandoned her, her living brothers she had lost track of, and she had lost the men she loved to other women. *What the hell!*

She also thought about her house. She still had a mortgage and owed about a year of taxes on the place. She pictured the bank and the city in a paperwork tug-of-war for the property; the bank wanting to sell it as a foreclosure to a real estate company; the city wanting to auction it off to a private investor for the taxes. That should be fun for them; it was a nice place.

In her jail cell that evening, Cora refused the one phone call she was told she could make, and spoke to the police woman who had offered her the phone; a woman who seemed to be of mixed race: "*I'll share something with you. At one time people are in your life, and at another time they're not; for whatever reason. They're okay and you're okay. Nothing about the planet essentially changes. The world keeps spinning 'round, and life keeps tumbling out at you. You're a young woman; just be careful not to ever get white paint on your forehead.*"

As the young police woman drove home that evening intent on stopping by the house of her mother who was suffering from severe depression, her white husband having recently divorced her for, according to her mother, no reason that she was aware of, the words she had just heard from that jailed woman started coming together in her mind; words that she had at first dismissed as mindless rambling. She wondered if those words would make any kind of sense with regard to the situation her mother was now in, her father having moved on to a caucasian female. Over the next several months, as she went about her life dating men both black and white, she found that she could not dispel that thought.

* * * * *